E-3⁵⁰

# THE SLAVE TRAIL

# THE SLAVE TRAIL

A NOVEL

BY

ALAIN GERBER

Translated by
Jeremy Leggatt

Mercury House, Incorporated
San Francisco

English translation copyright © 1989 by Mercury House, Incorporated. All rights reserved under international and Pan-American Copyright Conventions. Originally published in France under the title *La Trace-aux-Esclaves,* © 1987, Editions Grasset & Fasquelle.

Published in the United States by
Mercury House
San Francisco, California

Distributed to the trade by
Consortium Book Sales & Distribution, Inc.
St. Paul, Minnesota

Manufactured in the United States of America


*Library of Congress Cataloging-in-Publication Data*
Gerber, Alain, 1943–
  [Trace-aux-esclaves. English]
  The slave trail : a novel / by Alain Gerber ; translated by Jeremy Leggatt.
     p.  cm.
  Translation of: La trace-aux-esclaves.
  ISBN 0–916515–51–6 : $18.95
  I. Title.
PQ2667.E674T713     1989
843'.914 — dc19                                                    88-7844
                                                                          CIP

*To the Queen of Hearts*

Until a very short while ago the simple act of beginning a new paragraph filled me with indefinable exultation, however short-lived; but with the passage of the years I no longer feel anything. Where once there was something between all the lines, a cool, enigmatic deep, all has now dried up, leaving only white dusty banks.

KEN KAIKO
*Metamorphosis or Death*

## ★ 1 ★

Steeped in blackness, moaning, the island heaved basalt breasts skyward. Hectic vegetation seethed right up to the outskirts of the village.

Our trek had brought us to where the island's only asphalt road ends abruptly in the brush. We had camped within the moisture-swollen walls of a filling station that had never seen service. A hurricane, or greedy hands, had carried off part of the roof, the doors, the shutters, even the pump handle.

Behind and below us, the ocean beat furiously against granite cliffs. On the other side of the road the dilapidated entrance gate of a former plantation stood starkly against the sky.

Half a mile away on our left the last lights in the village — a garland of colored bulbs strung across the front of the general store — had just winked out. Clément Calderanz pulled the rum bottle from his rucksack. The flames of our campfire threw tawny lights on his lowered eyelids. Paul seemed lost in his own thoughts; Nathalie stood framed in the doorway, her arms tightly hugging her fragile silhouette, her face turned toward the moist air emanating from the forest.

I had lit the fire. Now I was kneeling by it, unrolling the tents and sleeping bags to prepare for the next storm (we had already gone through seven that day). I was the guide on our little safari, the Hemingway-style White hunter: scout, porter, interpreter, and, should the occasion arise, medical orderly.

It had been Clément's idea to hike the forty-odd miles of the old Slave Trail, feeling our way along its few surviving traces; he

1

had been obsessed with the idea since we first landed on this island, where we had originally intended to spend two days at most. More than half of the hoary old Trail had disintegrated into wilderness. I had spent a whole night struggling with historical maps, trying to reconstruct its meanderings. Then Clément and I had combed the bazaars of St. Elizabeth (the capital of this Lilliputian republic, which had gained its independence only ten years ago) for supplies.

Meanwhile, Paul and Nathalie had gone to visit the sinister Forcerie, the colonial-era penitentiary that had once served as barracks and sorting station for the Black "cargoes" arriving from West Africa. They described it to us later: leg irons and chains still lay there, corroded by rust and salt air, scattered haphazardly among the ruined debris inside. But I was too disturbed by the feelings aroused during our visit to the harbor stores to pay much attention to their story.

Clément had insisted on paying for everything. While he was doing that, I went on to the next store on our list, both to save time and to relieve my own embarrassment. Until he caught up with me, the storekeepers seemed willing enough (if not exactly eager) to sell me supplies, which clearly weren't in great demand. But as soon as his towering form appeared over my shoulder, as soon as they saw that haggard face, that intense gaze that seemed to be burning through his swarthy skin, their attitude abruptly changed; serving us grudgingly, with the greatest ill-will, they seemed anxious only to see us leave.

Was their attitude just another expression of the nebulous hostility we sensed in the streets outside? Ever since we had come ashore from the *Cornhill Missionary,* the color of our skin had drawn angry, even threatening looks. At the Christophe-Liberté, the only hotel on the island offering a semblance of cleanliness and comfort, there were muttered tales of tourists vanishing, knifed in the alleyways around the docks or sacrificed to cannibal deities resurrected the moment the last European administrator had left the island. The hotel staff, dripping xenophobia from every pore, brazenly spied on the guests.

But, although this atmosphere was oppressive, it didn't explain why Calderanz inspired more hatred among the islanders than anyone else.

At dinner in the hotel the conversation had turned to the northern bush country at the other end of the Slave Trail. Apparently the government had washed its hands of these barren areas, where there was nothing but mosquitoes and swamp to arouse official greed. According to rumor, that part of the island was controlled by a handful of people locked in a power struggle and backed by bands of hired thugs dignified with the status of militia. At night, sodden with rum, this rabble snored on its leaders' doorsteps, while inside (behind windows walled over to defend against attack), the lords of the north sweated with fear and fever beneath ineffectual ceiling fans, a revolver in each hand.

That, at any rate, was what we were told at dinner in the Christophe-Liberté that night by a blotch-faced man who introduced himself as a priest (although neither his clothes, nor his manner, nor his face fit the part). He had been wandering all over the island for the past thirty years. Constantly harassed, discouraged by an unbroken series of failures, he hoped to return soon to his native Holland.

He spoke French with a Dutch accent all right, but I didn't know what to make of his other claims. I was less wary of his slovenly dress and unclerical manner than of the contrast between his disenchanted look and the fervor of his words.

Clément didn't share my reservations. He was fascinated by what the man told us and fired one question after another at him. Although the Dutchman answered readily, his replies seemed extremely vague to me, as if he were subtly trying to perpetuate some mystery. The darker the picture he painted of the island, the more excited Calderanz became. Finally, in almost triumphant tones, my friend told the so-called priest about the expedition he had in mind.

At once the man raised both hands to his temples. His gaze retreated into his head; closing his eyes as if to focus on images etched deeply in his memory, he began to intone: "Ah, my friends! The north . . . the north! Concession Eighteen . . . the Mirror Swamp . . . mirror, yes, that's the word for it, all right . . . mirror of shame and disgrace . . . Lord! In the north you will see . . . you will see . . . The place is not of this world . . . . Believe me, I have just returned from there. What could you possibly find there, except — "

He broke off and looked fearfully around the room. I was watching him closely, but nothing in his face or movements suggested he was acting. His warning had chilled everyone at the table, except Clément.

The priest was sitting across from Calderanz. Impulsively he reached over and seized his arm. "Sir, have you ever heard of Colonel Paradise?"

Clément smiled indulgently. "I certainly have," he answered smoothly. "I have even talked with a young man who fought alongside him as a guerrilla before independence."

This revelation appeared to rattle the priest, but Calderanz either didn't notice or chose to ignore it. "Perhaps, Father," he went on, "you may know a man named Lombardi? A bit of a charlatan, but a most entertaining character — and an astounding grab bag of information. He's been combing these islands for years and years . . . ."

"I know him, I know him," the Dutchman muttered unenthusiastically, eyes riveted on his plate.

"The man I talked to is his assistant, Joseph, a very tall Black, skinnier than his own shadow."

"Perhaps. I — "

"What you're saying, Father, is that we should avoid this Paradise character like the plague?" Clément asked.

The mockery behind his words was obvious, even a little overdone. But our companion did not blink. He seemed lost in his memories once again. At least a minute went by before he spoke.

"Are you determined to go?" he asked at last, his gaze lowered as if he didn't dare to meet Clément's eye.

"More than ever."

The Dutchman sighed. "And this young lady will be going with you?" he said, nodding at Nathalie. Then, turning to face her: "Mademoiselle — Madame — forgive me, do you really intend to commit this folly? This—why not say it?—this sin? Think . . . think . . . I beg of you."

At that instant he caught the eye of a waiter hovering nearby, pretending to clear the table while he listened to our conversation. He shuddered and shrank back in his chair, his lips tightly compressed.

All my doubts about his veracity suddenly vanished. The fury on the Black man's face convinced me that the priest was telling the truth—or trying to tell it. He must have known a good deal of suffering on this island, suffering that had disturbed his mind and caused the incoherence that had made me—wrongly, I now realized—so suspicious of him.

"I can say no more," he whispered when the waiter had moved a few feet away. "But understand me! God in heaven, please understand me!"

Clément was still smiling. Nathalie seemed completely unruffled. I turned to look at Paul.

Fingers curled around the neck of a beer bottle, staring intently into the square of night framed in the gaping hole that served as a window, he was sitting in profile to me. I saw—or thought I saw—a man struggling to keep troubling thoughts at bay. But wasn't that exactly what I was trying to do, merely by looking at him? In fact, what else was Nathalie doing?

In that moment I realized that none of us would give up the idea of following the Trail. Yet I felt that, except for Clément, none of us had a very clear idea of what was driving us.

★ *2* ★

Eleven years older than me, twenty years older than Paul, Clément Calderanz was considered one of the literary lights of his generation. In France, anyway. To be even more specific, in certain Parisian circles.

Behind a screen of wit, which the French value so much more now than in the days when it flowed freely in their streets, he had set himself up as a cynic. His last work — a tongue-in-cheek study of the phenomenon of literary inspiration — had sold like a Harlequin romance.

Television had made the great man's face familiar in the remotest rural outposts of France. The permanently mocking expression beneath the carefully trimmed salt-and-pepper mane made him a natural media celebrity.

Behind this mask our friend poured his considerable talents into playing the public skeptic. With both the pen and the spoken word, he was the consummate ironist. The fluid elegance of his style made him the darling of literary lion hunters. And the lucid irreverence of his public quips kept his readers permanently piqued, while flattering them into thinking they were as intelligent as he was.

In diametric contrast, Paul was a silent, passionate soul eternally alien to frivolity. As a result, he prized that inaccessible grace in others — which no doubt explained his admiration for Calderanz. Their work set them even further apart. Paul dragged his words out only after painful gestation. In his battle to translate his inner contradictions into literary form, he wrote attenuated, disjointed pieces, his sentences weighed down and endlessly modified by a cargo of adjectives and adverbs. In defiance of every literary rule, he betrayed excessive partiality for the characters he created, with the result that he always destabilized the balance and flow of his narrative.

But only the younger man, not his older friend, could claim to be an authentic storyteller. I had always known it. Clément himself had finally realized it. And I would have laid odds — at the time, anyway — that Nathalie saw it too. Only Paul — with the naïveté that I found one of his most attractive qualities — seemed unaware of his advantage.

The two writers had first met five years ago, after Paul had sent Clément a short and emphatic note; in it he said he considered Clément one of the greatest living writers and requested an interview. At the time, Paul was putting the finishing touches to a series of short stories while completing a law degree that had never interested him. He swore he would destroy the manuscript if Clément did not consider it worth publishing.

"Tommy," Clément had asked me wearily, "why do people want to become writers? Why aren't you and I the last surviving representatives of the species on earth? Look what this guy's sent me to read. He claims they're short stories, but they remind me of a cat trying to claw its way out of a bag!"

And then he had shamelessly blackmailed his own publisher into putting out the book. No reviewer gave it as much as a line, but Paul was in seventh heaven. He invited us out to a restaurant far beyond his means and ordered buckets of champagne.

He didn't go back to law school after his summer vacation. He rented an apartment in our neighborhood and lived off small writing assignments he owed to Clément's sponsorship, because Clément carried considerable weight in the short story world.

Naturally, the love Paul felt for Nathalie was as ardent as it was platonic; and naturally he imagined that no one had guessed his secret passion.

Two years later, a story he had rewritten seven times from beginning to end met with pronounced critical success, despite one reviewer's reservations about the author's "relentless hair-splitting." His third book was welcomed even more warmly.

Once he had received Clément Calderanz's blessing, Paul began to aspire to public recognition — although he still refused to concede a single comma to public taste. His rising sales figures bolstered his optimism. In his ingenuous way, he rejoiced in it all, as if delighted to see the world in good order and virtue justly rewarded.

Clément's relationship with fame was quite different. I would say he relished the respect he received but did not himself respect his reputation. Equivocally, and characteristically, he intended to reap his just due in homage and praise — but he reserved the right to question its appropriateness. He even seemed to perceive it as a kind of insult.

So the ecstatic reviews of his essay on literary inspiration plunged the private Calderanz — the man who did not ham it up for camera and microphone — into a state of chronic irritation that his closest friends paid for dearly.

I was less puzzled by his reaction than most people. In the final analysis, the book was simply a clever compendium of clichés, dressed up by the author's vivacity to masquerade as new ideas. Following in the footsteps of a few dozen earlier writers (but with much greater grace and wit), he set out to prove that what we call inspiration is simply a convenient word with pseudo-mystical overtones hiding more or less conscious remembrance, plagiarism, compelling ideological models, and narrative structures as old as language itself: in other words, a whole cultural sweatshop humming away without the worker's knowledge.

The unremarkable nature of this thesis accounted in large part for the book's dazzling success. Clément's jokingly irreverent tone did the rest. The critics lapped up the ferocity with which our friend punctured writers' balloons — beginning with his own. A whole chapter of the book exposed the yawning gaps and hasty patch jobs littering the work of Clément Calderanz and relegated him to the rank of a minor practitioner with none of the qualities that transform a skillful technician into an authentic creator.

As though he were one of the most credulous of his readers, he had not written a single word since this brilliant, slashing attack. Nathalie bore the brunt of his gloom. We were all distressed. Sometimes he would lash out at Paul or me. Particularly me, I thought.

"Tommy!" he would cackle, slumped in his armchair, a bottle of cognac within reach. "Want me to tell you the truth? You're a poor Yankee slob mooning around Paris in search of a lost generation. In ten years you've written all of ten stories — some of which are at least three and a half pages long. Why don't you try writing commercials?"

These attacks always irritated his wife. Nathalie sincerely admired my stories. Even the grimmest ones, she said, like those describing the fall of Saigon, were permeated with a vulnerability and tenderness that reminded her of Chekhov.

The next day, Clément, more than half drunk, resumed the attack: "I know what it is, pal: you write with your feet because when you try to write with your ass the pencil keeps slipping out. Isn't that so?"

I didn't turn a hair. "The whole truth, Your Honor."

His eyes dropped, and he mumbled: "But I love you, you know that?"

"I know it, and I thank you for it, Your Honor. And I don't deserve it."

"Bah! Who deserves anything? Dear little Paul's the only one who still believes in that kind of crap!"

He drained his glass and said unexpectedly, not looking at me: "I'm just a dead weight on Nathalie — that's all I am."

Nathalie was sleeping at the other end of the apartment. We were alone in the living room. The best I could muster to answer this dramatic statement was a short disbelieving laugh.

He glared at me. "I know what I'm talking about," he rumbled.

"The cognac knows — and you're fool enough to pay attention."

Late that night the phone woke me.

"It's Clément, Tom. Listen, I didn't mean to hurt you. Did I hurt you, Tommy? I'm going through a rough time; don't know what's happening, but I can't seem to snap out of it. I wish I could get a grip on things, only . . ."

What did he want? I had guessed a long time ago that he was far from satisfied with his apparent abundance of talent. Over the next few days I was able to get him to talk a little, and I began to understand what was gnawing at him: once his essay was finished, published, and acclaimed, the murky question of literary inspiration had begun to torment him for real.

He had trained all his intellectual guns on the question, and only now realized that he had simply obscured it in his own eyes. His failure hounded him. Perhaps for the first time, a problem had resisted his ability to reduce it to an insubstantial puff of smoke. Something was not just perplexing but also frightening him. What he was feeling deep inside was nothing less than fear.

Clutching at straws, he read and reread books about great writers, as if these more or less diligent, painstaking studies might unlock the secret of the genius of Tolstoy, Flaubert, Thomas Mann. He combed through diaries, intimate journals, volumes of correspondence like a maniac.

One remark of Hemingway's in particular stopped him in his tracks.

"That's my problem, Tommy! I've always believed I could take a shortcut around experience. What a huge mistake. You, at least, never fell into that trap: just about everything you write is about Vietnam. Know what Hemingway said? He said you couldn't be a real writer unless you had been to war . . . Puzzling, isn't it? But I think I understand what he meant. In fact, it makes perfect sense: how could words possibly be more real — or even *as* real — as things, as acts? At first glance it looks almost simplistic, but if you carry it to its logical conclusion it's a remark that goes a long way, for a novelist . . ."

And another evening, after uncorking a second bottle of booze: "If I made a joke out of so-called literary inspiration, it was simply out of spite. I'm just a conjuror, Tommy. I make anything that bothers me vanish into thin air. But this time I can't do it. Inspiration isn't something you can kick around. It lives — without me and in spite of me. It lives in real writers. No, I know what you're going to say. Sure I can write! I even write damned well, in a way. But that's not the problem. Dostoyevski couldn't write at all, and Proust wrote a lot worse than people think. So? Look at their books, and look at mine! It's like comparing a neatly cropped photo with a landscape in full explosion. Why are my books so elegant . . . so harmless? Because nothing I say in them was ever whispered into my ear: I had to concoct every last word myself. You remember Paul's short stories? Good God! They might as well have been written by a pig dipping its tail in ink! Yet on every page, in almost every paragraph, there were one or two of those little items no man can ever invent himself, for the simple reason that he wouldn't even know how to begin. You too, Tom, you pull off that kind of thing — admit it. I've been writing for twenty years, and it's never happened to me. Why? Am I some kind of cripple? Where did I go wrong? Well, now I know the answer: I believed you could solve every writing problem with the intellect, through technical virtuosity. They call that the sin of pride, my friend! But not only that . . . I haven't had the courage to put myself on the line. That old crap about good and evil, you know what I mean? I wrote so I wouldn't have to live. But if you don't live, you don't write either, no matter how many pages you fill. You're always too damned clever; you always believe in too few things . . ."

In a restaurant a week later he brought up the idea of a long cruise to some part of the world none of us knew.

★ *3* ★

Paul and I were invited along on the express condition that not a single penny would come from our pockets. With this established, Clément transformed our jaunt into a marathon spending spree.

He booked the best seats on planes, the best berths on ships. He rented the finest cars, reserved the finest tables, ordered the finest wines. At a conservative estimate, the royalties on fifty thousand copies of his essay melted away on our travels.

"I'm getting rid of compromising evidence," he said with a roar of laughter.

From island to island we left a trail of bloated checks in our wake. Texas millionaires, outdone, watched us with envy. The natives pretended we were Texas millionaires and robbed our friend blind. It merely heightened his euphoria. He was literally growing younger before our eyes.

And then, out of the blue, Paul was bitten by the writing bug. At chic bars, in hotel lobbies, in museums, on the beach, even in restaurants, writing as rapidly as if taking dictation, he filled page after page of a fat soft-covered notebook that never left his side. He kept it rolled up and stuffed into one of his pockets. Clément poked fun at his frenzy; but Paul, his gaze elsewhere, scribbled away as if he had heard nothing. Jack Kerouac on Benzedrine could not have kept up with him.

Within five days Paul had finished a long story, which he read out loud to us after dinner on the deserted beach of our hotel, while I held a flashlight on the page.

It contained no trace of the stifled rage or occasional ponderousness we had come to expect from his writing.

The story opened with the last luminous and melancholy lines of Turgenev's *Sportsman's Notebook:* "In spring, partings are easy — in spring, even the happy feel drawn far away . . . Reader farewell! I wish you eternal good-fortune." (I knew those lines by heart, as I did the ending lines of *A Sentimental Education, The Great Gatsby,* and Stig Dagerman's *Games of the Night.*) Then, without any transition, Paul began to describe a house, a garden, and a river in winter under the snow.

The river was frozen over. A woman was walking along its banks. The narrator recalled a sled ride on the ice on a Christmas afternoon. He briefly touched on the history of a wooden bench barely peeping out from under the snow. The house seemed deserted. But you sensed that it too had a history, in which the bench, the river, the garden, the woman, the man telling the story, and several other people had played their part.

But what was that history? The further Paul read, the deeper the mystery became. And yet the more that history resembled our own: I mean the history of each one of us. Our own secret seemed rooted in it, giving it its strength. We knew the mystery would not be unveiled, could not be, yet we hoped for that miracle. We went on hoping right to the end, and even for a short while after Paul had stopped reading.

Each of us was looking inward. Something like a sense of propriety made me turn off the flashlight. Paul sat slumped on the edge of a deckchair as if stunned by what he had just read.

"It's like a subtle shading of blues," Nathalie finally murmured. Paul stared at her as if he had just become aware of her presence. But there was worship rather than surprise in his eyes.

Clément rose and took a few steps to the water's edge, hands thrust deep in his pockets; then he came back to us with a heavy tread and stopped on the other side of Paul's chair. Somberly, silently, he stared at the gently moving sea.

Paul clumsily closed his notebook, flattening it against his thigh with his palm. Smiling to himself, he studied the sand.

My two friends had their backs to one another; someone wandering along the beach at that moment might have thought they had just quarreled.

I myself couldn't think of anything to say; but there was a tight knot in my chest. Nathalie stared over my shoulder into the vast blackness of the night. That was all.

★ *4* ★

The next day began in exquisite softness.

Sometimes in these latitudes you get the feeling that the islands really do sway in the breeze in tribute to the images of the poets. Yet I had seen similar mornings as a boy by the East River, when the Brooklyn air took on the transparency of crystal and an innocent light purified everything.

We set sail aboard the *Cornhill Missionary* shortly before noon. During the crossing, Calderanz made friends with a little man in a white T-shirt and khaki shorts; his upper lip was copiously and permanently beaded with sweat.

A silent, elongated, skeletal Black man shadowed the little man's every step as he strutted about, pigeon-toed, pipe-smoking, a living encyclopedia of the islands.

He had their history at his fingertips; he knew every physical peculiarity among them; he was a connoisseur of their myths and customs, an avid collector of their folk songs, which he himself recorded out in the swamplands, using an ancient tape recorder. He was also an amateur psychosociologist, a would-be political analyst: waving his arms and wreathed in pipe smoke, he outlined for us his extraordinary vision of the islands' future.

Yet all these ideas were in reality mere trifles, for his real hobbyhorse (which he mounted at the drop of a hat and with an almost lecherous expression) was esotericism: what he called (his tongue snaking around his lips) "philosophy."

From what I thought I understood (I couldn't grasp all of his ramblings), his system was based on the idea that the human mind had created (and was continuing to create) the material world; it had invented man himself, man in the flesh, and, as a result, world history had been nothing more than the enactment of a long epic poem.

The little man's name was Mr. Lombardi. He had once sold mail-order reed organs to planters' daughters; now he roamed the islands peddling a patent medicine of his own invention for lumbago. Everyone on board, except Clément, avoided him like the plague.

It was from Lombardi's fertile lips that our friend learned of the existence of an old Slave Trail on the island where the *Cornhill Missionary* would be dropping anchor late that afternoon.

In fact, we had scarcely settled into the Christophe-Liberté when Clément led us all down to the bar to announce his project. Later I marveled at our passive acceptance of the idea — as if it were the most natural thing in the world for a journey begun in luxury and high style to end in an ordeal worthy of Jack London's pen.

★   ★   ★

It was almost five the following morning before I finished working with the maps and documents Clément had handed me after dinner that first night in St. Elizabeth (he must have rushed down to the local tourist office, which closed at five o'clock, almost the instant the *Cornhill Missionary* docked). Exhausted, I fell asleep in the middle of my paperwork.

Clément came to wake me at nine so that we could make the rounds of the stores. Something about his appearance made me

frown as he loomed through the fog of my interrupted sleep. It
was a while before I realized that a crew cut (which looked as if it
had been hacked with a sickle) had replaced the mane that had
become his public trademark.

Gulping down a quick breakfast, we walked out into the "heat
and dust," bludgeoned by the sun's glare the instant we crossed
the hotel threshold. It took us hours to gather everything we
needed, particularly the all-important tents.

Early the next morning, leaving our luggage and most of our
belongings with the hotel receptionist, we set off with the priest's
blessing.

How could I have suspected the man? No one looked more
like a poor decent devil of a Dutch priest, forced to return to the
orderly tulip fields of his homeland in order to rediscover his
faith in Divine Providence.

Clément shocked me by laughing in the man's face.

But the old man found time to draw me aside and whisper,
"Sir, you seem more reasonable than your friend; please remember this advice. Avoid Colonel Paradise. That man is not—"

He was unable to go on. Several hotel employees had moved in
silently and were eavesdropping. He was panic-stricken when he
noticed them. The Blacks really looked as if they were about to
do him violence.

I felt so sorry for the unfortunate man that, when he gave me
his hand a moment later, I gripped it longer than was necessary.

Tugging on my arm, he brought his cheek close to mine and
without moving his lips muttered something I didn't catch.

When I pulled free, I realized that he had slipped something
into my palm; I hastily stuffed it into one of my pockets. Already
he had become a pale silhouette, half swallowed by the gloom
inside the Christophe-Liberté. The employees gathered on the
steps outside were looking at us now not with hatred so much as
derision.

★ *5* ★

We left St. Elizabeth by a path scattered with garbage, skirting the ruins of a nineteenth-century hospital built on the corner where the road from the port to the Forcerie had once forked to give birth to the Trail. The beginning of the Trail had disappeared, but it started up again a little farther on, disguised as a local road.

Three miles outside the capital, a farmer bent over his crops straightened up to wave at us. Pleased at this show of friendship — in such stark contrast to the reception the islanders had shown us so far — we eagerly returned his greeting.

The farther north we went, the friendlier the natives became. They might even have turned out to be downright hospitable, if we had been looking for hospitality. But we preferred to limit our contacts with them to practical necessities. We bought what we needed, paid the asking price without haggling, and camped at a respectful distance from the villages.

Yet Clément's appearance still troubled the islanders. Their eyes veiled over, their faces closed; they were suddenly in a hurry to finish our business. Every time it happened, it startled me. And since it seemed hard for Nathalie to bear, I decided to take full charge of our supply runs, on the ground that this would be a fairer sharing of the workload. As a result, I began to get a feel for the dialect spoken on the island.

Ever since independence, firearm sales had been unrestricted in St. Elizabeth. Clément, after asking my advice, had bought four Smith and Wesson revolvers in the market there. We kept the guns holstered and buried deep inside our packs. We would take them out and wear them once we reached areas where (according to guidebooks published thirty years earlier in Europe) wild animals still prowled.

Rifles or shotguns would have suited our purpose better; but to keep them out of sight we would have had to dismantle them — greatly reducing their effectiveness! I had been against carrying them openly, slung over our shoulders. We would be entering an area where hunting had been forbidden ever since the tragic death of a St. Elizabeth café owner. Displaying weapons could have signified only two things, both undesirable: either that we had hostile intentions toward the natives, or that we expected hostility from them.

The Trail kept vanishing into thin air. Luckily I had bought a wrist compass, which I was wearing on a leather strap. Inevitably it reminded me of the compass that had often led me back to base after a firefight had scattered my platoon in the jungle. To satisfy a whim of Clément Calderanz's, I suddenly realized, I was once again confronting a situation I thought he had liberated me from forever.

Very soon after the end of that war I had realized that I couldn't go on living in the United States (it would be years before I could even think of living there again).

I was the survivor of a lost war, a war condemned by the best and the brightest of my compatriots; for a time I dragged myself around the decaying neighborhoods and rusty streets of Brooklyn, a borough every bit as rundown as I was.

I would have had to share this purgatory with too many ghosts reminding me of earlier years of promise: a whole procession of haunting memories escorting the funeral march of a civilization I had believed in heart and soul without realizing it. I had the feeling that I was living—if "living" is the right word—the last days of America, of an America that would never be the land of beginnings again.

It was as if that America had been merely a mirage looming out of the Atlantic mists before the startled eyes of adventurers ready for anything, but as naïve as children. And now, in a distant war that she herself perceived as an unholy abomination, America, the land without a past, had given up on the future.

My mother had done a lot of her growing up in Europe. So I went to Europe; and Europe generously offered me the consolation I craved.

It was obvious at first glance that Europe's worn-out nations weren't going to find their youth again any more than America was. But I found this reassuring: their destiny seemed to be to preserve their memories and their illusions, the obsolete certainties and the even creakier uncertainties of the White race, at any price — even at the cost of their own creative energy.

Europe was slowly wearing herself out: the process had begun long before her birth, under Grecian porticos and in arrogant Byzantine schools. She was wearing herself out, but she wasn't collapsing. America, it seemed to me, was nothing but rubble. Gutted mausoleums.

My mother was the daughter of a Canadian Embassy official who had insisted that his family speak French as well as English. She had lived in Paris for more than twelve years before she married. Because of circumstances (and my father's modest income — he was athletic coach at a school by the East River) she never returned to France. But she often talked to me about the neighborhood where she had lived in Paris, near the Jardin des Plantes. Thanks to her, I was comfortable enough with both languages to be able to think in French when I finally found myself in French-speaking company. But it was really because of the pleasure it would have given her (if she had still been alive) that I decided on Paris rather than Vienna or Rome.

To tell the truth, nothing much else counted with me. It wasn't the reality of the Old World that had lured me from home. In mourning for America, I remained thoroughly American, obsessed by the myth Americans have created for the benefit of other Americans.

Admittedly, the everyday Europe I lived in had nothing in common with the Europe of the guidebooks and encyclopedias; but it was still a storybook Europe. Or at least a literary Europe. All I really wanted was to walk in the footsteps of Hemingway, Miller, Scott and Zelda, Kerouac's *Satori in Paris*. I strolled around the city. I inhaled its smells, drank in its music and its lights. Yet it never ceased to be a place of the imagination for me.

And because imagination never lets itself be bothered by the facts, I basked in a leisurely life-style that had long since deserted Paris, in a *douceur de vivre* that probably never had existed, in a mythical urbanity daily contradicted by the behavior of the vast majority of Parisians.

I needed this blindness. To purge myself of American violence, I needed to believe in the manners of the Old World; I saw evidence of refinement everywhere — when all that had really survived was a vestige of the conventions, stripped of content and intent: no more than tics, in fact. But to my eyes they were new . . .

A well-to-do American couple let me live in a studio apartment they had. One day at their home, I met Clément Calderanz.

Writing the kinds of books he did, he seemed to me to embody the very essence of Western culture, as I imagined it, the way I imagined everything else.

I had no idea what he saw in me, but we were immediately drawn to one another. A few weeks later he introduced me to Nathalie; from then on, I had dinner with them almost every night in their apartment on Rue Notre-Dame-des-Champs or in one of the last genuine Montparnasse bistros. No neighborhood suited me better. I was living the pages of *A Moveable Feast*. I was working hard to defuse my memories of Da Nang and other places.

Without realizing it, Nathalie was an enormous help. I was attracted by her serenity and — if that's the right word — her spontaneity. As saturated as I was with American vulgarity, I particularly liked the fact that common words and gestures were out of place around her. Yet she was always marvelously discreet; her good manners, her "class" were as natural as her good looks.

Paul and Clément (obeying a typical writer's impulse, although writers hate the proliferation of books) both encouraged me to write; but it was Nathalie's wordless approval that gave me the courage to confront the blank page.

★ *6* ★

I could feel the object the priest had slipped me slapping against my thigh as we walked. An odd reticence prevented me from pulling it out of my pocket in front of my companions, but I had been wondering about it since we set out. I waited until I had a chance to examine it in private, screened by a stand of mango trees.

All I could tell before I looked at it was that it was a small sharp-edged object, astonishingly heavy for its size.

What I saw in the hollow of my palm was a tiny statuette, probably made of platinum; its base was a plinth not much more than half an inch square; it was about an inch tall. It was the edges of the plinth that I had felt through the lining of my pocket during our march.

The figurine itself was of a naked woman with long hair tumbling down her back. No more than an inch in height, she was holding an open book.

I raised the object closer to my eyes and began to pick out details so tiny that they had escaped me at first. Across her eyes the diminutive, enigmatic reader wore a blindfold no thicker than a hair.

The more closely I examined her the more I was puzzled by the allegory. No sooner had I seen the blindfold than I discerned the faintest ridges in the metal of the woman's wrists.

Could they be bracelets? If so, they would have been massive, given the delicacy of the small figure. One idea led to another, and I wondered whether the artist had meant to indicate hand-cuffs, some kind of restraints.

I would have needed a powerful magnifying glass to verify this theory, and even then, differentiating between handcuffs and bracelets on such a minute scale would probably have been impossible.

I put the statuette back in my pocket and came out from behind the trees. I was puzzled. I tried to persuade myself that the failure of his spiritual mission on the island had unhinged the Dutchman's mind and that I should not attach undue importance either to the scene at the hotel or to the gift he had given me. Perhaps he had just slipped me the first object that had come to hand, as a kind of souvenir. But that still didn't explain what such a worldly object was doing in a priest's pocket.

## ★ 7 ★

Chafing to be back on the Trail, Clément Calderanz merely picked at his food. It was as if he had already arranged some mysterious assignation up ahead.

Yet at noon the sun over the Trail was unbearable. We were in no hurry. We were even a half-hour ahead of the tentative schedule I had worked out back at the hotel.

The place where we had stopped hung over the emerald and violet waters of a small creek edged with black sand. Nearby, three traveler's-joy trees spread fronds like enormous monstrances. The rainy season was late. The Caribbean basked in all its gentle glory, its presence filling the air around us with a memory of vanilla, of cocoa, of cinnamon and brown sugar.

Clément was indifferent to it all. His gaze, dark with preoccupations I could only guess at, was riveted inland. I was amazed how much this man, my closest friend, had changed in the space of a few days.

The cropped hair had given his features a drawn look; in certain lights his skin had the waxy hue of death. And at the same time he seemed to be burning with unfamiliar fires, with a secret passion that made him inordinately irritable. Where was the sorcerer, the wag, the irrepressible cynic?

As I wondered about this curious change I saw him grope for his sack and pull it toward him. He took out a notebook with a pencil fastened to the cover with a brass clip. He immediately began to scribble feverishly. But after less than a minute his pencil stopped moving.

Methodically, Clément slipped it back into its clip. He ripped out the page he had just scrawled, rolled it into a ball, changed his mind, smoothed it out again, and finally tore it into four pieces, thrusting the fragments deep into a breast pocket. Slowly, his eyes focused on the real world once more. The light burning in them went out like a candle flame.

He looked at us one after another, first wearily and then — it seemed to me — with irritation. Sighing, he shoved a hand back into his sack, pulled out his sleeping bag and unrolled it.

Inside was a bottle of rum. One look told me that Nathalie was as surprised as the rest of us. I thought she turned pale when Calderanz (after each of us had refused his offer of a drink) downed a good quarter of the bottle at one swallow.

But she quickly pulled herself together. It occurred to me that this woman, who looked so vulnerable and who attached so much importance to the fragility of things, was almost certainly made of tougher stuff than the rest of us.

That fall, she and I had taken a walk together in the Luxembourg Gardens. Faulkner set the epilogue of *Sanctuary* there: "across the pool and the opposite semicircle of trees where at sombre intervals the dead tranquil queens in stained marble mused, and on into the sky lying prone and vanquished in the embrace of the season of rain and death." After that, every time I looked at Nathalie I saw her as she looked to me that day, almost transparent in the sun's rays.

It had been raining all morning, and the opal light softened sharp angles, muted harsh greens, bathed everything in impalpable shades of gray, beige, blue, and ocher. There was no denying it, Paris was aging badly. But she was still one city — I didn't know many others — capable of reinventing herself on the right day in the eyes of those discovering her in innocence. And I loved her for it.

I loved those old gardens after the rain. I loved those early February twilights that bathe the quiet solemn housefronts on the Rue de Médicis pink under a golden sky. Saigon at that moment seemed very far away. Better still, it seemed beyond recall. Paris, on the other hand, was a place where you could walk aimlessly with a woman by your side, where your hands might brush by chance, or where you might simply imagine such a thing happening.

Nathalie had arranged to meet me to talk about Clément. It was at the height of the crisis following publication of his essay.

She was worried about him and worried that our future relations would ultimately be destroyed by his attacks on Paul and me.

"Perhaps Clément is not a very good friend to you, Tommy, but you are the best friend he could possibly have. Paul can't help him — quite the contrary, I'm afraid. Which shows how badly he needs you. Please try to be patient."

I was stung. "Patient? He's my friend! I love him."

"Yes," she said. "Love him. You must love him."

We had stopped in the middle of a path and were facing each other. The silence between us became so laden I would never forget it; nor would I forget the unexpressed yearning of that moment.

We walked on a little, and she asked: "Why do most writers hate themselves so, Tommy?"

"I guess it's a question we all ask ourselves. There may be one explanation, but I'm not sure it's worth much . . ."

"I'd like to hear it anyway."

"Okay . . . Well, if you don't have enormous self-esteem, if you're not convinced you're the very best of the bunch, you can't even begin to write — unless, of course, you're a complete asshole. So you start to write. But then you quickly come up against a dilemma: the more esteem you win (assuming you're lucky), the harder it is to hold on to."

"I don't understand."

"I mean, the first thing that happens when you become pretty good is that you discover how much further you still have to go. And the further you go, the further your goal recedes. There are good things to be said about this state of affairs, but for a writer it's almost unbearable, because he constantly disappoints himself; he becomes incapable of making progress. Silly, huh?"

"But you're not like that."

"I'm worse! Believe me, I have more pride than a writer needs to write. That's probably why I write so little. A good writer can't love himself, yet people are always forcing him to pretend he does: the public requires writers to be monsters of vanity or else it doesn't take them seriously . . . That reminds me of something. Over in Vietnam I was nobody's friend. And nobody was my friend, except a musician named Thelonious Monk. I always had a Monk tape on me, even when we were out on patrol. Sort of a good luck charm. Strange thing to believe in during that war! You clung to anything and everything. Why not Thelonious Monk's harsh music? It was the most incorruptible thing I knew. The most solid thing, at a time when everything else seemed to be melting away . . . Monk died without knowing how much I loved him. Would that have helped *him* not hate himself, I wonder?"

We walked in silence to the grill separating the Luxembourg Gardens from the Observatoire neighborhood.

Inexplicably, all the past sorrows that I thought were dead and buried were churning inside me again. Once more I was confronted with old, long-forgotten defeats. That day I was stripped of my European illusions.

Yet the Avenue de l'Observatoire was a place I would have liked to see live forever. Somber, vaguely melancholy, and in a way slower than the rest of Paris that I knew. As if it still held the voices of the children who had played there at the turn of the century; Marcel Proust would have described them without ever seeing them, because *he* didn't need to see. That Paris hadn't aged; and it hadn't tried to grow young again.

"I think Paul would be capable of not hating himself," said Nathalie, "if he had someone who believed in him through and through."

I had nothing to say to that.

When we reached the Closerie des Lilas, we spotted Clément sitting at a terrace table with three girls, Danish students with dazzling complexions, who had recognized him on the street.

He was speaking, and they were taking notes with a lot of loud laughter. Nathalie drew me to another table.

A year later, on the shores of the Caribbean, Calderanz recorked his bottle of rum and shoved it back into his sack.

A man, almost naked, appeared by the little creek. There were violet highlights in his dark gleaming skin. He strolled down to the sea, his face turned toward us. I had the feeling he had been spying on us for some time before emerging from behind the coconut palms.

Clément's back was turned toward him. I was about to warn him when he hooked his thumbs into the straps of his rucksack and gave the signal to move out in a voice that was not to be questioned.

★ 8 ★

As I had hoped, our first day's march was fairly easy. It was Paul I was worried about; physical stamina did not seem to be his strong point.

I had planned on doing the trek in short stages, and we were still in the most civilized part of the island — the area with the best roads, the safest area, and the area blessed with the healthiest climate. Mosquito eradication campaigns were launched periodically by the local health authorities, but we had been warned that we would lose the benefit of them once we had passed the village of La Lanterne. Beyond lay the north, a zone (if we could believe the priest) left to its own devices by the government in St. Elizabeth. The road we were now on, begun before independence to link the northern and southern extremities of the island, also petered out in the region of La Lanterne.

Scattered here and there along the Trail (and sometimes smack in the middle of it) were small hamlets, the distances between them increasing the farther we moved from the capital. They rarely boasted more than a dozen dwellings — plank and sheet metal shacks very like those in the shantytowns of the capital. But nearly every village had a bar and general store, invariably better stocked than its outward appearance led you to expect. Most of them even had pharmaceutical products, periodically restocked, which meant we had set out loaded down with many things we could have bought along the way just as easily, and often more cheaply.

In these subtropical regions, the sun sets early and twilights are brief. As soon as the light started to fade we had to start thinking about pitching camp. Our first job was to gather enough wood to keep a fire going all night. That was why I had allowed generously for the unexpected in planning the successive stages of our trip.

Since we hadn't encountered any particular obstacle that first day, we reached the place where we were to spend the night shortly before four in the afternoon.

Clément wanted to capitalize on our head start by pushing on. I had a lot of trouble persuading him that we had nothing to gain by upsetting a schedule designed to ensure optimum travel conditions. After all, I had to remind him, this was an outing, not a forced march. He merely grunted sullenly. But Nathalie backed me up decisively, while Paul took no interest in the argument, as if its outcome were of absolutely no concern to him.

With extremely bad grace, Calderanz yielded to his wife's reasoning; it affected his mood for the rest of the day.

A few hundred yards from our tents a sluggish sea lapped the shore. He refused to go swimming with us. When we returned to the camp he was seated, his face savage, his gaze absent. His notebook sat closed on his knees. He pretended to ignore us, while we tried not to look at the rum bottle on the ground beside him, two-thirds empty.

The remaining third vanished with our meal.

For a long time we sat in silence around the fire, avoiding one another's eyes even when we had to pass food. Only Paul seemed immune to our general ill ease. For that reason perhaps, Clément finally turned to him and said (as if we had spoken of nothing else since the meal began): "About that story of yours . . . you know, that, er, that tapestry of fugitive gleams and muted murmurs" (he stressed these words maliciously) "something about it bothers me . . ."

Paul, usually so eager to hear the older man's opinion, did not even raise an eyebrow. He simply waited; this seemed to irritate Clément even more.

"There's no vision of hell in it!" he exploded. "Nothing but blue — wasn't that it, Nathalie? Why not shove a little red into it as well? What kind of writer do you think you are if you shrink from confronting evil? And I mean evil, my friend, not just a couple of nasty little habits and a few grownup fantasies!"

He laughed unpleasantly through clenched teeth. Nathalie rose in a single swift movement. For the first time I noticed that trick she had of hugging herself. For a second, stopped in his tracks by her reaction, Calderanz looked as if he might get hold of himself. Several times he blinked. But finally he returned to his attack on Paul, who still hadn't moved a muscle.

"You used to have more guts! Could you be getting cold feet, Paul? What's frightening you, kiddo?"

"Not you, if that's what you're wondering. No, not you anymore."

"Are you absolutely sure?"

"Not anymore. Never again. But let me return the favor: what's got you so scared, Clément?"

There I was, witnessing this absurd scene, hearing this ridiculous dialogue. But I couldn't believe my senses. How could things have deteriorated so fast? For two days I had been living at close quarters with these two men, who also happened to be old friends, yet I had not felt the mounting tension. Was I really so obtuse?

Now Calderanz was brandishing his notebook. "A real book is a report from hell," he snarled. "Nothing to do with the kind of literature that tickles the ladies' fancy!"

Nathalie sat frozen, staring into the dark, while Paul, as if to stress his utter indifference to Clément's heckling, gazed steadily at her back.

Feeling totally excluded from the intrigue that had developed among my friends, I wanted at the same time to find out all about it and to know nothing about it. Many things suddenly changed at that moment. I foresaw that our journey was not going to be one of enlightenment but of dark revelation. It was my turn to be scared.

When I turned in, I felt as though the most private fibers of my being were brutally recapturing the memory of certain Vietnamese nights, when fear took possession of us but our hearts mysteriously overflowed with a kind of wild adoration.

Was I getting back in touch with old demons too? As my senses grew steadily and almost unbearably sharper, plunging me wide awake into a nightmare of larger-than-life noises and smells, I rummaged through my pockets in search of the figurine. The blindfolded reader, the prisoner of night . . .

In the morning, the sharp corners of its plinth were almost embedded in my palm.

★ *9* ★

As soon as he opened his eyes Clément complained that he had slept badly. He grumbled that he needed a darker darkness to find sleep.

To make matters worse, the insect-repellent cream the rest of us had used with success had not prevented colonies of mosquitoes and other creatures of the night from parading over his face. He therefore decided to make himself a mask that would protect him both from the light and from the insects.

The object he fashioned defied description.

Amalgamated from the unlikeliest materials (including clumsily shredded clothing and pieces of metal crudely hacked from food cans), it was a kind of helmet with a movable visor, a soft floppy article stiffened with metal pieces that clicked at his slightest movement and added to the overall barbaric effect. With the visor up, the hood looked like the hybrid offspring of a ski mask and a gas mask; for eyes it had two circular openings lined with tin that had been made to bite into the cloth with violent blows of a hammer.

I had seen very similar abominations at the anthropology museum in Paris in the exhibition of African ritual garb. A red cotton sportshirt, cheerfully sacrificed, provided the dominant color.

Clément tried on his mask.

Anyone else decked out in this fashion would have been ridiculous. But there was no denying he had a certain style. The general impression was intimidating, if not downright threatening: sort of like the aura that hovers around a genuine witch doctor.

As soon as we had finished our coffee, we started out again. The day was going to be a scorcher. We needed to take advantage of the morning's relative coolness for the first few miles.

## ★ *10* ★

On the third day we reached an area just short of the village of Sémillance, where brutal overseers working for the planters had once carried out their most atrocious crimes.

Leg irons, gallows, and other instruments of torment and execution had once stood along the left-hand side of the Trail at this spot, their arms outstretched to embrace the poor devils who had in one way or another provoked the anger of their keepers.

The overseers had been recruited from among ruined settlers, dockyard scum, rebels, deserters, criminals. Body and soul, they were ravaged by bad liquor, venereal disease, and every kind of tropical rot; they knew they would die without seeing their native land again, without regaining the smallest measure of self-respect. These tragic wrecks had no consolation other than the sufferings they inflicted, with unbridled ferocity, on the slaves — as though they sought to observe in others the effects of the torments awaiting them in hell. The only curb on their sadism was the planters' need for a steady supply of manpower in fit condition to work.

But their ruffled and bewigged masters concurred that strict discipline over the slave convoys was essential. It was understood that a certain percentage of the cargo was inevitably lost or damaged during the long ocean crossing or on the road from St. Elizabeth to the various large inland estates. And until the French Revolution the price of a slave was low enough to allow a certain amount of spoilage.

The torturers extorted their sinister tribute from this human mass. They went about it with fierce joy, first in the Forcerie, where excessively proud necks were forcibly bent, and then in this camp at Sémillance, deliberately set up for the infliction of punishments decreed after the slaves had left the capital.

Scenes of butchery took place here in broad daylight, accompanied by laughter and jests, ribald songs and drunken vomiting.

They didn't just punish real or imagined crimes, they also degraded their victims through pain and humiliation. One after another they raped everyone who could be raped, most often using weapons, tools, bottles, or sticks — since vice and the unhealthy climate had undermined the virility of the executioners.

After that they finished off the wounded and the sick, who were cheaper to replace than to heal. This gave rise to new orgies of horrors. The slaves were flayed alive, hacked to pieces, castrated with bare hands; the debauchery continued through the night, each refinement of cruelty drawing its inspiration from the acts preceding it.

Then came the first slave uprisings. In Haiti, after bloody convulsions, Toussaint-Louverture, Dessalines, and then Henri Christophe established a Black nation. On the island of St. Elizabeth, troubles broke out in the plantations in the north and spread down the Trail to the southern tip.

For reasons still unclear, the insurgents (who could easily have reached the capital and perhaps made themselves masters of it) stopped short at the Sémillance slaughterhouse, where we now stood.

But this was not the only thing that puzzled historians. Reading the material Clément had given me that first night at the

Christophe-Liberté, I learned that the revolt had caused very few deaths among the White population. Fewer than thirty in all, and only one woman. These were probably the only ones the slaves were unable to capture alive — scattered, defiant groups who had not been taken by surprise by the howling tide but had barricaded themselves in their mansions with their weapons, inflicting heavy casualties on their attackers. There was even reason to believe, from survivors' accounts, that a dozen had taken their own lives.

Not the least extraordinary aspect of the affair was the fact that the Blacks, instead of slaughtering their former masters, submitted them to an ordeal that was repeated nowhere else in the islands.

With the full agreement of their men, the leaders of the uprising decided to take as many prisoners as possible and bring them to this torture camp.

The terrified captives assumed that they themselves would now have to endure the treatment formerly inflicted here in their name and in the name of efficient work. A quite different fate was in store for them.

The mob merely knocked down the grisly instruments of torture; then, after the ringleaders had conferred, they formed a circle around the area where the Whites were huddled.

There then began the extraordinary entertainment that would last the whole of the next five days — until it was cut short by the arrival of a heavily armed relief column, which had marched up from the capital without striking a blow and met no resistance at all from the rebels. Not as if they were resigned to defeat but as if they had taken some hypnotic or hallucinatory drug. It was — as the naval officer leading the column put it — as if a "blissful dream state had overtaken their minds."

Threatening their prisoners with the direst punishments, the slaves had forced them to become the actors in an astounding theatrical performance. In return for their lives, the prisoners treated the mob to a faithful, convincing reenactment of all the ceremonies, rituals, games, and passions that had one by one cemented and divided colonial society.

There were sham marriages, trials, balls, duels. There were parodies of banquets, counterfeit funerals. There were concerts with silent musicians scraping make-believe fiddles. A wordless tragedy was solemnly performed. The audience was even treated to the sale and punishment of slaves.

At first the insurgents seemed highly amused by these playlets (either because they were new to them or because they were all too familiar). But little by little their laughter gave way to astonishment, then to distress, then to fascination. The show went on all day and all night, many observers going without sleep so as to miss nothing. They stood there gaping, unable to tear their eyes from this theatrical act of hallucination.

At the same time, as if they were caught up in the game themselves, the unwilling actors stopped asking their captors what themes they were to improvise. They chose their own subjects, often by tacit consensus, and, as the days wore on, their imagination and spontaneity came to the fore.

The will to live — and fear — certainly fueled their zeal. So did the rum, which flowed freely and helped both actors and spectators to keep each other going (since more substantial food was lacking). But there was something else.

The best-informed commentators were unable to shake off the conviction that a phenomenon akin to collective hysteria (although clearly a mild form) had taken hold of the actors. The Whites themselves were hypnotized by the images they had created of their own lives, as if they had suddenly realized the paltriness of their former pretentions, their ephemeral glitter, their impenetrable foreignness — everything that made them the garish emblems of satanism in the eyes of their human cattle.

Of course, the reprisals that followed the uprising were of unparalleled brutality. But more than one settler lost his mind as a result of this strange episode. Others hastily sold off their goods and went back to where they had come from. One big landowner, long notorious for the harshness with which he ran his estate, left wife and children to join the Franciscans. There were rumors of little bands of slaves who managed to escape the reprisals and took to the hills, where they carried on the ritual of the Great White Theater to the sound of drums and the drone of a complicated liturgy.

More than ever, the camp at Sémillance lived up to its reputation as a Caribbean garden of torments. It would remain so until the middle of the nineteenth century.

★   ★   ★

Not a trace of it remained. Not even the foundations of the guards' barracks, even though they were still marked on the most recent of my maps (dating from the next to last year of the colonial administration). Most likely the masonry was still there, but vegetation had swallowed it.

The Trail itself was invisible at this point — which perhaps explains how a battered van came to be parked smack across the path.

And, since the tourist trade had long since withered away on this island, its owners — a young man and woman seated on one of its running boards — did not bother to hide their astonishment when we emerged from a tunnel of vegetation thirty yards in front of their faces.

★ *11* ★

The dreams Michelle and Julien had shared were so beautiful they were bound to be shattered.

They had been trainee teachers in a dormitory city in the Paris area; they had asked to be assigned to humanitarian duties (like the Peace Corps) in this young republic as part of France's far-reaching scheme of aid and cooperation with her former colonies. Their request had been granted: they were the only applicants.

One fine morning they stepped ashore from the *Cornhill Missionary,* hearts pounding, drunk with good intentions and enthusiasm. But they had scarcely set foot in St. Elizabeth when their ardor was put to a severe test.

No one was expecting them. They gathered — although no one ever said it outright — that neither the local authorities nor the French consul had been notified of their arrival. To add to their bewilderment, the same consul even tried to dissuade them from getting in touch with the Ministry of Public Health in St. Elizabeth; he suggested (although in the most circuitous way) that they would be well advised to leave the island at once.

Shaken by this reception, they nevertheless persevered in their appointed mission; their attempts to make some kind of official contact led them from one closed door to another.

At last, outside what looked like a deserted shed in the dockyard area, they were left to fry in the sun for hours under the guard of a huge ragged lout who trained his automatic pistol on them whenever they tried to speak to him.

Around noon they were herded into a room where they couldn't help noticing a blackish liquid spattered and dried all over the walls.

Poker-faced officials examined their papers with ponderous care, scrutinized the official statement of their mission, then went out into the corridor to confer in low tones before return-ing to inform them dryly that they were not to leave the capital without written authorization from the police. They were then dismissed, or more accurately thrown out.

They wrote letters of polite and veiled bewilderment to their superiors. It was as if they had not written: no one replied. They suspected the local administration of intercepting their mes-sages. St. Elizabeth's only two public phones, located at the post office, were out of order, which eliminated this means of com-munication. No one in St. Elizabeth's tiny European colony would have invited them to his home, much less allowed them to use the telephone. Moreover, it was rumored that all phone lines (there were fewer than twenty on the island) were bugged; their owners used them for calls strictly related to their business or their everyday needs.

What most distressed the two young people was the attitude of the White community. They seemed to be considered undesirables. They were treated like lepers.

The consul himself received them with reluctance — and then only if they happened to catch sight of him on his veranda and it was impossible to have his wife tell them he was away.

On these occasions he gave them information so evasive and so halfhearted it merely increased their bewilderment. He was obviously holding something back. His wife never had the courage to look them in the eye.

One day they handed their country's representative a written distress call — couched this time in the most explicit terms — with the request that he pass it along to the French Foreign Ministry. He picked the letter up with the tips of his fingers as if it were a particularly loathsome object, and for the next several weeks he remained out of sight. When they finally caught him leaving the Christophe-Liberté he wriggled out of their grasp by pleading an urgent appointment at the presidential palace. All they got from him was the surly injunction to "remain at the host government's disposition until their contracts expired." But they were never shown a written order, signatures, official stamps.

The consul was also supposed to pay them their salaries. But he would pull their money out of his billfold without a statement or receipt of any kind; and certain of his highly ambiguous comments could be taken as suggesting — although why would he have done it? — that he was paying their expenses out of his own pocket.

Still faithful to their mission, however, and not yet cured of their trustfulness, they offered their services everywhere. Everywhere they were more or less politely shown the door. Each time, however, someone took the trouble to remind them that they were not to leave the capital. After that they were simply turned away as soon as they approached the reception desk.

That wasn't all. They soon had the vague sense of being watched, spied on. Wherever they went they were followed. Or at least they felt certain they were. Often, though, they would subsequently see this or that imagined spy busy at the most innocent occupation: carpenter, delivery boy, barman, itinerant watermelon vendor.

The first Christmas they spent on the island was the darkest day of their lives.

When they came to draw their monthly wages from the consul they were a living picture of dejection.

The sight of their lifeless eyes and bowed heads merely irritated the man. "Of course," he grunted, "you too imagined these islands would be a branch office of paradise! How ridiculous! Oh, I'm not blaming you for being naïve; where you come from they do everything they can to keep the idyllic vision alive. And while the people here were still under our yoke, they had no choice but to act the part of overgrown children who wanted only to laugh, dance, and lounge about in the sun wearing picturesque rags. Lies that helped them to put up with us, and to survive. But do you really think they enjoyed it? No more than any poor bastard anywhere who has to keep smiling for the benefit of those who control the purse strings. To be driven by need to act the clown: what fate could inspire greater hatred in a human being? There are no more minstrel shows here — and there never were any! The songs, the clothes, the bright lights, all that existed only in the imagination of the tourists. They thought they were seeing reality, but all they saw in fact was a bunch of advertisements brought to life for their entertainment. The show's over — what did you expect? It's a very different kind of show they're putting on now!"

He suddenly broke off, looking anxiously over his visitors' shoulders as if afraid he had said too much. "But you should have figured this out long ago. What irresponsibility! And now here you are," he grumbled, thrusting them out into the street.

Michelle and Julien stumbled away with the feeling that their strongest beliefs had been undermined. They did not even have the courage to share the bleak thoughts the official's sermon had provoked in them. Both pretended not to notice the man following a few yards behind on a rusty old bicycle.

From that time on they were tailed night and day. Curiously, though, they sensed that the natives they were in contact with —

the small shopkeepers in their neighborhood — were beginning to show signs of friendship.

A short while later a dilapidated jeep screeched to a halt outside the "cabin" the consul had allocated them. Three soldiers leapt from the vehicle and burst into the single room of their makeshift lodgings, weapons at the ready. Behind them came a civilian in a white double-breasted suit, thin as a skeleton and so tall he had to bend double to avoid crushing his navy blue homburg as he crossed the threshold.

Without bothering to introduce himself, or to remove the long American cigarette dangling from his lips as if it were smoking itself, he informed the two teachers that the authorities had decided their presence in St. Elizabeth was undesirable.

For an instant Michelle and Julien wondered whether they were going to be summarily shot. Instead, it was suggested that, "in order to maintain the excellent relations enjoyed by our two nations," they move to the north of the island and there try any experiment they saw fit, cultural or otherwise — on condition that they not attempt to return to the capital.

As he explained all this, the man conducting the operation went through every conceivable shade of expression from disapproval, arrogance, sarcasm, pity, and condescension, to irony. He actually seemed to be gauging each of his effects, as if a camera had been set up in a corner of the room to immortalize the scene.

Timidly, Michelle reminded him about the dark rumors circulating about the area where they were being sent. The man in the felt hat twisted his lips into a smooth smile: half bantering, half sneering, he told them that educated people had no business listening to gossip scarcely worthy of market fishwives.

But that very evening, just after nightfall, the Black man who had followed them from the consul's residence propped his bicycle in their yard and without further ado warned them — if they ever wanted to see France again — not to go farther north than the place called Three-and-Two-Clouds. Then he straddled his machine and pedaled furiously away.

The incident seemed so unreal that the young couple almost doubted it had taken place. The next day a man they had seen repairing nets in the port—easily recognizable by the khaki raincoat he wore over a naked torso and ragged shorts—came to tell them that they could have the use of a van that had once been used as a traveling library and that still had its full stock of books.

Luckily Julien was a good mechanic. He put the wreck they were shown into operating condition. Michelle repainted it sky blue.

The damp climate had affected the books; many had rotted. Overall, though, the teachers felt the books might prove extremely useful. Moreover, when they went over the contents of the library, the young couple had a number of pleasant surprises, particularly a bound collection of works from the eighteenth and nineteenth centuries. They decided to consider this discovery a sign from fate: fortune's first smile since they had stepped ashore from the *Cornhill Missionary*.

After a curious incident (which disturbed us when they described it to us—I'll come back to it later), they turned their backs on the stagnating city that had witnessed their disillusionment and headed north, overflowing with a whole new set of illusions.

Their reception in the outlying villages—whether friendly, indifferent, or hostile—seemed to be determined by ups and downs beyond their comprehension. After a few weeks they decided to stop worrying about it and to dedicate themselves exclusively to the work they had come here to do.

Their open-air classes attracted few pupils. Fewer still, they soon learned, could even write their own names. But if they were saving few people from ignorance and superstition, at least they felt that they were fighting the good fight, that they were no longer completely useless. Little by little they rekindled the fantasies that had brought them so far from home.

They decided to pass up the two months' annual leave in France stipulated in their contracts (and which neither the consul nor anyone else had so much as mentioned). "Perhaps we're not teaching them anything," they kept telling each other, "but we're learning so much from them."

There was some truth in this. What they learned was a measure
of both their ignorance and their zeal. They studied the island
flora and fauna: herbs, trees, insects, reptiles, birds whose very
names they had never heard before. They studied the esoteric
domain of rites and religions. They absorbed the island's twin
histories: the one written by the White settlers and the one the
slaves whispered to each other through legends and songs that
their masters tried in vain to stamp out.

After leaving St. Elizabeth, they had crisscrossed the island
from coast to coast, covering a patch of land thirty miles long and
about twenty-four miles across. They were afraid to stray any
farther south than the point where they could see the city's
"suburbs," in case the police picked them up. And they were
reluctant to go any farther north than La Lanterne, the last stage
before the hamlet of Three-and-Two-Clouds.

Beyond lay the malevolent north, which most islanders mentioned only in a whisper. No one tried to stop them going there:
people simply took a malicious pleasure in throwing out enigmatic hints that could have been either warnings or threats — or
even, as their supremely elegant policeman had claimed, simply
figments of the popular imagination.

Sometimes the islanders hinted that the whole region known
as the Mirror Swamp, which lay around Concession Eighteen,
was peopled with creatures who assumed human form only in
daylight hours. At other times, they stressed the all-too-human
ferocity of the local guerrilla leaders and their murderous militia.
Pressed for more definite answers, some natives simply fled.
Others seemed struck dumb by the implications of the questions
put to them. Two or three simply roared with laughter.

The couple were no more successful when they tried to find
out what had become of the consul. It had been agreed that, at
the end of each month, he would remit their salary through one
of the few White men still living in the interior of the island: the
owner of a small backwoods market in the village of Sansoupir.

When they had gone to see him the previous November, the
man had told them, with obvious reluctance, that there had been
"a problem." What kind of problem? He was not sure. There was

no way of finding out. The consul was no longer at his post. But the island authorities had agreed to keep the young couple supplied. They could take everything they needed at the market, as they had always done. At the end of their tour of duty the value of these purchases would be deducted from the wages due to them. Naturally, there was no official document to confirm the validity of this arrangement.

They could get nothing more out of the storekeeper, who clearly wanted them out of his store even if they removed all its contents without paying him a cent. Needless to say, they did not take undue advantage of the proposed plan. Not just because they were honest but also because the terrible destitution around them made it impossible for them to flaunt the relative prosperity the arrangement would have brought them.

So the French consul's post was vacant. Seeking to clear up this new mystery, the young people were once again presented with a tangle of conflicting answers. Edouard Mercier had been recalled to Paris. Edouard Mercier had succumbed to a sudden illness. He had been arrested for espionage and was being held incommunicado. Extremists had kidnapped him. Some also said he had only been a phony consul anyway, and that the French government had always refused to accredit him. The real consul had been Mr. Lombardi—but Lombardi could not stand the climate in the capital and had always preferred to live in the interior.

No sooner was one such revelation proffered than another was put forward to contradict it. Michelle and Julien finally decided to ignore the rumors proliferating around the island. This helped them regain faith in themselves, and it rid them of the anxieties that had been so deliberately and painstakingly cultivated in them.

"And now," they told us, "we're cured. No more fairy tales!" From now on they wouldn't allow themselves to be intimidated by the irrational. After all, their honor and dignity were also at stake: weren't they the enlightened representatives of lay education in an island that seemed poised to slip back into obscurantism?

From now on nothing would stop them. They would ignore the horror stories. They would explore the north of the island. Hadn't the Sansoupir storekeeper assured them (although in the most circuitous way) that they would see their native land again? And who had given them that assurance? The very people who denied the authenticity of the horror stories.

Dawn the next day, they told us, would find them north of Three-and-Two-Clouds, as long as there was even the hint of a trail for the bookmobile to follow.

### ★ *12* ★

But what about the strange occurrence that preceded their departure from St. Elizabeth? I said earlier that I would deal separately with this episode because it made such a strong impression on all of us.

Just as they were climbing into their vehicle to leave the capital, a man had appeared: a purple-faced character between fifty and sixty years of age. The young couple were sure they had never met him before.

Although his appearance lent no credibility to his words, he introduced himself as Father Hendrik Van Doren, from Vlaardingen in Holland; he was about to return to his native land after thirty years on the island.

Showing signs of the deepest agitation, shooting furtive glances in every direction, the stranger asked the teachers if anyone had ever mentioned a certain Colonel Paradise to them. When they said no, he abandoned all reserve and began a long breathless plea: on no account were they to go anywhere near Concession Eighteen. The place was like an antechamber to hell, he said, and the colonel himself—a monster of perversion, slave to a brand of depravity so horrible it could not even be named— was more demon than man.

Van Doren's demeanor was so wild—at times he shouted, at times he whispered in barely audible tones—that the young couple believed they were dealing with a madman. They promised to be careful, thanked him for his kindness, and hastily drove off in the bookmobile.

Later, when they questioned the natives about the colonel, their confusion was inevitably compounded by the usual sequence of yeses, noes, and perhapses; the natives giving free rein to all the resources of that singular art in which they were past masters: fog-shrouded allusions, lucid but totally contradictory hints, stubborn silences, anguished silences, stunned silences, sudden withdrawals, sly smiles, great bursts of hilarity. As always, the teachers finally gave up trying to get an answer, telling themselves that in the final analysis the natives' behavior was merely harmless, meaningless clowning.

We would probably have been of the same opinion if this Van Doren had not subsequently delivered an identical message to us. As I listened to Julien's description of the priest, I automatically slipped my hand into the pocket where the figurine lay. I was almost tempted to ask the teachers if the priest had given them anything. Just in time I recalled that my companions knew nothing of our furtive exchange on the steps of the Christophe-Liberté. And until I solved the mystery of that statuette myself, I preferred to keep things that way.

Moreover, when our eyes met, I realized that they felt no more inclined than I did to reveal to the young couple what we knew of Hendrik Van Doren (if this really was that strange character's name). Our reluctance to tarnish the enthusiasm they had so painfully rebuilt probably played a large part in our attitude. But I am afraid that murkier motives were also at play. An obscure hesitation to force destiny's hand. Curiosity about what would happen now that the elements of the intrigue were in place. This attitude is common among writers—who are voyeurs by necessity, but even more so by vocation. Behind a screen of highly plausible rationalization, they readily sit back and watch the most unbearable events run their course.

Whatever our motives, we said nothing. But I noticed that Nathalie and Paul were as astonished by this story as I was.

Clément Calderanz, on the other hand, looked as if he were at a party. He was positively radiant. He almost winked at us. Every time the couple related some new mishap he was visibly delighted, retaining barely enough moderation to stay within the bounds of decency.

When Michelle and Julien had finished their story, and the meal we had shared was over, he proposed a toast to the success of their endeavor. We all raised our glasses. Then he confirmed that Lombardi had indeed been consul once, but on another island.

"We know him only by name," said the young man.

"A pity," said Clément with a private smile. "You don't run across visionaries like him every day . . . Having said that, I don't believe he's as crazy as some people say. And even if he isn't quite right in the head, his view of the world is of more than passing interest to me."

But when we asked him about Lombardi's intriguing world-view, he merely said tersely that, as far as he knew, it represented the only form of idealism that magnified reality. The clear implication was that he did not care to elaborate for peasants such as ourselves.

"He understands more things than he believes," he concluded. "The opposite of Kant and Hegel, so to speak."

The young people laughed lightheartedly. Not knowing Calderanz, they could not appreciate all his twists of character. They took what he said at face value. So the insolent pleasure he had displayed while listening to their story had passed right over their heads.

Admittedly Clément had turned the full battery of his charms on them ever since we had reached the clearing, a thing he often did with strangers (Paul and I both knew something about that). Few people were able to resist him in this mood. Moreover, although we still had several miles to cover before reaching the place where we were scheduled to eat our next meal, he had insisted that we halt here and share our lunch with the two young people.

A second toast followed the first, then a third — and so it went until the bottle was bone dry.

Fairly drunk by now, the teachers urged us to take a look at the bookmobile's shelves. We climbed in. (I forgot to mention that, while making the introductions, Clément had deftly avoided giving his own name. Nor had he said anything about our literary activities.)

Suddenly he rapped the spines of three volumes. "Well, well, well. What on earth are you doing with these?"

It was dark inside the bookmobile; Julien had to lean close. "Clément Calderanz," he read in a low voice.

"Clément Calderanz! That aging choirboy!"

Flushing to the roots of her hair, Michelle jerked around.

"I can't say he's my favorite writer," said Julien, "but you're not really endearing yourself to my wife: she considers him a genius."

"A genius?" Clément snorted. "Who knows? What do you think, Paul? Is Clément Calderanz a genius? No, my dear young friends, come on, that would surprise my friend here and me a great deal. But there's one thing we can tell you for sure: the man is no novelist."

"The man," said Paul in a loud and clear voice but with no particular intonation, "is a finished author."

Despite the distance between us and the fading light I saw Nathalie start, her face crumpling, her body trembling from head to foot. Clément had fixed burning eyes on Paul, but they held more provocation than real anger.

Suspecting nothing unusual in the situation, the young couple were undisturbed by this exchange. Backed by her husband — who jumped to the rescue whenever needed — Michelle had begun a learned disquisition whose argument rested on examples taken from Calderanz's writing. Clément, who had turned his back to us, set about demolishing their arguments with ferocious wit. I saw from Nathalie's expression that she was making a tremendous effort to hear none of it. Meanwhile, Paul was glaring at what he could see of Clément's profile.

The argument might have dragged on indefinitely if the three participants had not finally agreed that Calderanz's essay on inspiration was really no more than a pleasant diversion.

" 'Detour' would be a better word," Paul broke in.

He had been unable to hold back; but he must have tried. Turning to look at him, I saw the sweat rolling from his temples to his chin. I would have given a lot to know what he was thinking.

"Detour!" shouted Clément with a pain and violence that startled the two youngsters. "Detour, yes! Retreat! Treason! Perdition!"

"Dispossession," said Paul, still staring at the ground.

"No!" the older man shot back. *"Lack* of possession. I said *possession,* mind!"

"Abdication," Paul muttered.

"Abdication? Never!" Clément yelled, whirling to face Paul. "Never, you understand? We— This Calderanz rushed like a fool into the trap that his whole life's work had set for him. So now you say he has no alternative but to keep his mouth shut, is that it? So we can relegate his work to the rank of drawing-room prattle? Why not? And what if he's come to the same conclusion himself? Why wouldn't he decide to close the book on all that and commit himself to a new direction?"

"Such as north," said Paul, still staring at his toe caps.

"Who gives a damn where?" yelled Clément. "So long as it's not polluted by purveyors of fugitive gleams and muted murmurs. They'd avoid it anyway if they had an atom of sense—it might upset their sublime elegance, their precious sensitivity . . ."

"But here I am" was Paul's only reply, in such low tones that I was probably the only one to hear him.

Michelle and Julien were shaken by the storm they had so innocently unleashed. They had no idea what to say to save the situation.

"Perhaps Clément Calderanz will quite simply carry on publishing books like the ones here," Julien suggested to break the silence.

"Not a chance!" my two friends retorted simultaneously, one angrily, the other contemptuously.

Nathalie was hugging herself.

With a small embarrassed laugh, as if all this were just a joke in rather poor taste, Michelle drew our attention to some of the old books they had found on the library shelves. Julien joined in with enthusiasm, proudly displaying a volume of medium thickness, bound in tobacco-colored leather and once decorated with gold leaf (just a trace remained on the rosette stamped in the middle of the cover).

"Look at this!" he said, his delight somewhat forced. *"Account of My Voyage to the Isle of Indecisa and of the Things I Saw There,* by the Abbé Descamps, Bordeaux, 1779. Did you know that this country was once known as the Isle of Indecisa, or Indecisa Island, until the English occupied it at the beginning of the nineteenth century? Strange, isn't it? As if the people who discovered it were uncertain about it and wanted to record their uneasiness. Anyway, from what I gather, this book is the only one devoted exclusively to the island: a unique document, in other words! Unfortunately this copy isn't in very good condition, but you can guess your way through the illegible sections. I've read it so often I know it almost by heart. Here!"

He held it out to Clément, but the writer (with a reluctance close to repulsion) refused to touch it. It was Paul who took the volume and opened it, while Nathalie, as if a stranger to what was going on, climbed out from behind us and stepped down from the bookmobile.

At first Paul glanced through the book carelessly. Then a passage seemed to catch his attention. He turned back a few pages and began to read attentively. Clément watched him impatiently from beneath his eyebrows, with all the signs of mounting rage.

"Well?" he finally exploded. "Do you think we're going to watch you jerk off all night? Are you learning to read, or what? Maybe that's what you should go back to."

"What are you reading that's so fascinating?" I asked to distract Paul's attention.

But my diplomatic intervention was not necessary. From Paul's quiet gaze and almost childlike smile, you would have sworn he had not heard Clément's insulting words.

"It's not so much the story as the way the story's told," he answered delightedly. "This priest had a way with words. Just listen to this one paragraph:

These black heathens, although bent beneath a yoke of fearsome toil and often beaten by their masters' janissaries, fall to singing on the smallest occasion; and so immoderate is their taste for barbarous grimace and display that they flaunt the depravity of their nature for all to see, giving themselves over to pantomimes bearing little kinship to reason and still less to humanity. They love nothing better than to vex the world by deeds and by a demeanor that oblige one to enter into their game, only to perceive very shortly that this game is sheer absurdity; they themselves would be hard pressed to discern what profit lies in it, much less its motives or ends. Despite the misery of this rabble, worship of fetishes is held in high regard among them. They turn in veneration to grotesque idols represented by bits of wood, shreds of leather, the tail of a beast, and other such base trophies. They also cherish vain and extravagant beliefs, holding, for example, that the moon enters into carnal commerce with them, and most particularly with their wives and daughters; and that the souls of the dead visit them, bringing them much trouble and great torment, because the spirits are (so these people say) malign in character; and yet they sometimes take pleasure in the beating of drums, which these people and their turbulent dead prize more highly than our subtlest and most cunning harmonies. Their thoughts, their gestures, all conspire to suggest that they contemplate the divine creation only after sealing their eyes. Thus, carrying elucubration to its furthest limits, they claim to heal the sick through a whole array of impertinent and shameless tricks, most often dishonest, practiced at the patient's bedside. Furthermore, they consider themselves, alone among the races and nations of earth, capable of foretelling the imminent demise of a man in seeming good health, simply by gazing upon his countenance; yet by a strange paradox they derive more distress and confusion than pride from this gift . . . .

He slowly closed the book, his eyes lost in a dream that, to judge from the softness of his expression, must have been very sweet to him.

"Ah, Tommy!" he murmured after nodding several times. "What wouldn't I give to have written, just once, something like 'their turbulent dead' . . ."

"It would be great, kiddo, if the dead were all we had to worry about," Clément said sourly.

The young people looked at each other in dismay. Fifteen feet away, outside Clément's line of vision, Nathalie was packing our things. I suddenly noticed that she was rummaging through Clément's sack. She pulled out the notebook, looked rapidly through it, and replaced it. I turned away, embarrassed at having caught her in the act.

Paul had come back down to earth. He was glaring at Clément. "The dead no longer have the right to speak," he said distinctly, his jaws clenched, an ugly light in his eyes.

I really thought Clément was going to attack him. But once again, despite her bewilderment, Nathalie had enough presence of mind to intervene.

"The strangest thing," she said in a high voice that shook a little, "is that the Abbé's description hasn't lost its validity over the last two centuries. Of course, people's thinking has changed. The slaves were freed. The Caribbean finally suffered the backlash of the Industrial Revolution that had so shaken Europe. But here more than anywhere else the Blacks remain connected to their roots."

"And independence," Julien cut in, "marked the beginning of what we Whites would call regression — but which was perhaps just a return to the fundamental values of an ancient culture. In a sense Africa is more immediate here than in Dakar or in Timbuktu. Since this is one of the poorest islands in the whole Caribbean, very few White people ever settled here. Now most of them have left; obviously their influence was so superficial it flowed over the Blacks without leaving any traces, or virtually none."

"It's hard to believe, I know," Michelle added, "but after spending a few months traveling from village to village we've had to face the facts: life here doesn't have any of the dimensions familiar to us. Although it will probably make them poorer than ever, the islanders have turned in upon themselves. Upon their myths. Upon a vision of the world that has nothing in common with that of their closest neighbors . . .

"In fact, they haven't the slightest interest in what happens outside the island. It's as if the rest of the planet were merely a fable to them, a passing mirage. That explains their attitude toward us, I suppose: they treat us like little children to be amused or lulled to sleep with stories. Sometimes the stories are funny, sometimes frightening. It doesn't matter which, as long as we leave them in peace and don't try to understand matters too grownup for us.

"They don't even have any interest in the policies of their own government! There haven't been any elections since independence. No one knows who's in power in St. Elizabeth, or what he does with that power."

"Everything's falling to pieces," added Julien. "Everything's rotting. It's almost as if the human environment obeyed the same laws as nature. The people work only just enough for subsistence. Their poverty gets worse with every passing day, and nobody gives a damn. The country has sunk deep into stagnation, but strangely enough it's a happy stagnation—a kind of bliss, reminiscent of Africa before it became the arena of struggles for spheres of influence among the powers and an international bone of contention. Do you think a single one of these islanders worries about the future? No! They behave as if time were just a moment that stretches infinitely on, without the smallest prospect of progressing toward a new state of affairs . . ."

He stopped. None of us wanted to speak anymore, it seemed to me. Which of us hadn't dreamed at one time or another of stopping time? What was writing, if not an attempt to realize such a dream?

It was past three. Against all our expectations, Clément

accepted the offer of a lift in the bookmobile for the distance we would have covered on foot if we had set out again on schedule.

His face betrayed fatigue, or more accurately exhaustion. He went off obediently when Nathalie put her arm around his shoulders and told him his rucksack was ready.

"Yes," he said dully, "everything's ready, I guess."

But a little while later, in the bookmobile, he absentmindedly wriggled out of her embrace and began to examine the rows of books with a look of derision, as if throwing down some kind of challenge to all this literature.

Nathalie was avoiding my eyes; she sat with her gaze fixed on the back of Paul's neck as he squatted, fists on hips, watching the brush go by the bookmobile's side window, which had been shattered by some projectile.

The strange bad blood between my two companions seemed to me to augur bad times ahead. As I tried to restore a little order to the thoughts tumbling around in my head, I realized that for some time my right hand had been clenched around Father Hendrik Van Doren's statuette.

And I was suddenly startled to realize that the allegory, while still obscure, had lost a part of its mystery. The myth of the blindfolded reader found an echo in one of the sentences that had particularly struck me in Abbé Descamps's description: "Their thoughts, their gestures, all conspire to suggest that they contemplate the divine creation only after sealing their eyes."

I thought again of what the platinum woman held in her hands. An old-fashioned phrase came into my mind, probably a remnant of childhood reading: "The Great Book of Creation."

★ *13* ★

The air still had not cleared by the time we took our leave of the young couple. Only Clément Calderanz seemed preoccupied with other things: it was obvious he wanted to get back on the Trail. Our good-byes were a bit strained.

The bookmobile went off into the wilds.

After a half-hour's march through open country under a brutal sun, it became obvious that we had eaten and drunk too much to keep up that pace without ill effects. But Clément refused to consider any change in our plans.

We trudged on painfully, and the shacks of Sansoupir finally appeared at our feet in a crease of land.

I went down to buy the few things we needed. For a moment I thought of asking Paul to go with me, hoping he would enlighten me about his falling-out with Calderanz. But I was too tired to face such a conversation. There would be other opportunities. Besides, did I really want to know what he was thinking? Did I really want answers to my questions?

In any case, it was going to be hard to forget our encounter with the two teachers. Already, the appearance of this village seemed to confirm what they had been saying: it looked exactly like an African village magically transported across the ocean.

Down in the basin where it huddled, a pocket of heat seemed to have been accumulating since the dawn of time. Going into it was like descending into a volcano. A vibrant silence plastered the dust of the village streets to the ground, like the ashes of a demolished world. But I sensed eyes watching me from the depths of the huts. Telegraph poles trailing mildewed pieces of wire were a melancholy reminder of the passage of another civilization, noisy but ephemeral.

An indefinable aura, not quite a threat, hovered in the air. A kind of expectation. Something intense and brooding.

The local store stood out with its roof of sheet metal (rusty, of course). I went in and for nearly a minute was alone. Then a man with defeated eyes emerged slowly from under the counter. A White man, or what was left of one; he gave off a sickening smell of sour beer: clearly the teachers' supplier (although the young people had avoided describing either this character or his whereabouts).

All kinds of unwanted articles were fermenting and decomposing with a stale but pervasive stench against the walls and on the ground, while vitally necessary goods were sorely lacking. But the man appeared not to give a damn about the success of his business.

His eyes kept leaving my face to study something over my shoulder. I resisted the temptation to turn around, even though he probably wouldn't have noticed if I had.

I had heard about this kind of human flotsam, left high and dry from the colonial era, men no longer capable even of homesickness. They had lost faith so completely that despair itself was foreign to them. They no longer believed in God or the devil, in life, in humanity, and least of all in themselves. They were encamped on the battleground of their defeat, swaddled in their white skin as if it were the sullied shroud of all desires and all hopes. In their own eyes, in everyone's eyes, their death would have no more meaning than their life: both rested beyond sadness and joy, in that desert of the soul where time alone still throbbed in its endless death throes.

Uneasier than I cared to admit, I got through my business as quickly as I could, confining my exchanges with this man to the strict minimum.

The tropics, I thought, as I watched him drag himself from one shelf to the next, are a vast, sumptuous lie. The glittering sky presides over splendors secretly hatching their own destruction. What the duped visitor sees as the apotheosis of life is in reality its cancer. In the short or the long haul, it is always putrefaction that conquers — after surreptitiously winning the hearts and minds of too credulous humans.

Converted by the sword and contaminated by the verminous freight of the trading ships, the original inhabitants of these islands had died out practically without trace. The islands proved more compassionate to the Blacks, who had fertilized the land with their blood. But the children of Europe would always be interlopers here, despite their quinine and their smugness about their accomplishments. They had no more place here than in the

Asian domain that had just witnessed their defeat, certain of the final outcome from the moment they had set foot there.

In these kingdoms of dissolution, nothing was adulterated and corrupted as quickly as the White man's will, his pride, knowledge, and power. I already felt — too vividly for my own comfort — that I had been plunged, like Joseph Conrad, into the heart of darkness. What madness had compelled me to go along with Clément's whim? And what about him? What demons were driving him?

I was beginning to have some idea; but perhaps it was not too late for us to get a grip on things . . .

As I was leaving the village, a slender form dashed behind a hut, a fleeting image in a floating scarlet dress whose metallic ornaments had flashed in the sunlight, catching my eye.

Obviously I had seen something I wasn't supposed to. Something was brewing in Sansoupir.

But what did it matter to me? I had already spent too much time under this island's spells. I went my way quietly, forcing myself to keep my eyes straight in front of me.

The overheated air was suffocating. The supplies weighed a ton. I had to stop several times to catch my breath. The others were waiting for me at the prearranged spot.

★ *14* ★

What I had assumed from the map to be a natural clearing turned out to be a circular arena about fifty yards across; it had been carefully cleared of grass; stakes had been planted all around it, five or six feet apart. They could not have been much more than six feet tall; I could touch their tips by raising my arms above my head.

I had no idea why, but there was something deeply oppressive about this mysterious configuration. My companions had felt it too before I arrived: they stood as far from the stake perimeter as they could.

Although we were no longer in the Sansoupir basin here, it was still baking hot. A mother-of-pearl strip, extraordinarily pale and glittering, formed a bar at the western horizon. I had never seen anything like it in my life.

I busied myself with my various tasks. No one wanted to talk. I considered ways of getting Clément to turn back. I knew — without overestimating my importance — that he could not hope to go on without me. Would he insist on continuing if I threatened to quit?

Throughout the meal (it was short, because none of us was hungry), Nathalie kept looking hard at me. What message was she trying to send? I couldn't make it out. But when I wandered over to a flamboyant bush after the meal and she followed me, I was not surprised. Clément was taking long swigs from a fresh bottle of rum.

He had asked me, or rather ordered me, to bring him a bottle from Sansoupir. And to tell the truth, it had not even occurred to me to disobey, even though it would have been easy to find an excuse. Why so much deference to a man who was no longer himself, who needed to be protected against his own impulses? What confused motives were driving me? Maybe Calderanz was not the only one who had changed . . .

★   ★   ★

I heard footsteps behind me. It was Nathalie; she was staring intently at me, and I was struck by the seriousness of her expression.

"Tommy," she said in a tight, controlled voice. "You're thinking of deserting him, aren't you?"

I stiffened. "Deserting him?"

"Please, let's not play with words. You've made up your mind to leave him, haven't you?"

"I don't know yet. Frankly, I ought to, but—"

"Without you he'll never make it."

"I don't think so either." I swallowed. "Wouldn't that be better? I don't know exactly what's going on in his head, but he has to give up this madness while there's still time. Don't you agree?"

"He won't give up!" she burst out. "He won't give up whatever you do. It's you who have to give way. Tommy, I beg you."

The bush was restless. The night seemed like a huge dark hand about to close on the island; to crush it, as if age-old alliances among the elements had just been overthrown.

I felt myself losing resolve before the light in those magnificent eyes; distress made her gaze even more compelling.

It was my turn to beg. "At least tell me what he's after! In just a few days he's become almost unrecognizable! As if he were bewitched. It wouldn't surprise me if we all were. Look at Paul. And at me, for that matter. If I were a nineteenth-century novelist, I'd say this island had cast an evil spell on all of us. We have to break it at all costs. You're the only one who can help me."

Still looking deeply into my eyes, as if she had heard nothing of what I was saying, she simply repeated: "Don't desert him, Tommy."

My whole body hurt with the effort not to take her in my arms and hold her tight against me. I armed myself with a show of inflexibility, hoping it would be enough to sidetrack her.

"I've got to know what's going on," I said, trying to make my voice sound hard. "You must understand, Nathalie: I can't fly blind in a business like this. You are the only true friends I have. I feel as responsible for you as for myself. And I have every reason to be worried, after those vicious exchanges between Paul and Clément. I don't understand what's happening to us, and, until someone explains it to me, I refuse to play any part in it."

Her eyes had not left mine. They had simply retreated behind a veil (of disappointment, I thought, or of embarrassment; but as soon as she opened her mouth again I knew it was something else). "Are you so sure you don't understand?"

I couldn't help blinking. I thought I heard mockery behind her question and felt my face turn red. "I understand that we're

ruining this trip, and by doing so we're compromising everything
that held us together," I said stiffly.

"Perhaps," she murmured. "But can't you see what Clément's
obsessed with?"

"All I can see is that he is obsessed."

"Really? Nothing more?"

"Really. But I have to admit I haven't tried hard to figure it
out."

"You're a writer like him, Tom."

"Not like him, no. I wish I were."

"You wish you were? Is that true? Have you told him so?"

"I have too much trouble admitting it to myself!"

"Then all this is your business too, whether you like it or not."

". . ."

"We wouldn't be here today, waiting for something, or scared
of something whose nature is a mystery to us, if Clément had
gone on believing in what he was doing. That damned essay on
inspiration—everyone thought it was just another think piece,
when in fact it was a confession. If he was using it to settle old
scores, he was settling them only with Clément Calderanz."

"I think Paul and I both realize that."

"Then you diagnosed the disease: it wasn't all that difficult.
But you didn't see how deep the disease went. At the first
encouraging sign you thought everything was fine again. You
believed that, Tommy, don't try to tell me otherwise."

"I wanted so much for it to be true."

"I'm not reproaching you: so did I. But we had to be extremely
careless to let ourselves be taken in by his act: such a surge of
good spirits coming after so much rage and bitterness—it just
wasn't possible. The very idea of this cruise—coming from a man
who claims to hate traveling—that should have given us pause, to
say nothing of all the other whims he's subjected us to. When a
man has been wounded to his very core, wounded in what
justifies him in his own eyes, he can't recover so quickly. Wounds
like that never close completely."

"Wait a second . . . You spoke of Clément justifying himself
just now . . . He has an incredibly lucid brain. How would it

justify him in his own eyes to think he had the imagination of a Dickens? He has to know he never had that!"

"No, Tom. For him, justification lay in thinking that a writer could do without that very quality, that there were equally respectable — I could almost say 'legitimate' (in fact, he used the term one day) — forms of literary creation. That's what he has lost — that assurance, that shield. And, in losing that, he has suffered the cruelest mutilation that an artist, or a man —"

She turned away suddenly, unable to go on. Now I felt guilty for not drawing her to me to comfort her, the normal reaction in situations like this. But I knew that if I even touched her . . .

"I want you to understand what I'm trying to say, Tommy," she resumed in a voice I was relieved to hear was as firm as ever. "Those aren't just words. What Clément has lost is not just confidence in himself or respect for himself but his strength, his power. His drive. What made him live . . ."

"But all three of us saw him turn the corner, back in Paris and then in the first weeks of this cruise . . ."

"He believed he had found the solution to his problem. His inspiration (remember what he told you that night?) would be the fruit of out-of-the-ordinary experiences. Obviously he wasn't going to out-Hemingway Hemingway and join a mercenary squad. But at least he could leave his ivory tower and live fast, loose, and dangerous, turning his life into material for a 'real-life' novel he would later put down on paper. The stranger the facts, in other words, the richer the fiction. At first, things didn't go too badly. He armed himself with patience. He was lucid enough, as you just pointed out, not to expect a couple of adventures and a few exotic images to transform his life into a novel and turn him into a master storyteller. But he was on the lookout for every opportunity for stronger stuff."

"Enter Mr. Lombardi!"

"Lombardi isn't the only one to blame, unfortunately. By the time they met, Clément would have clutched at any straw thrown him by any glib talker. At least I think so. We were the ones who failed him. Especially me . . . And then on top of everything, by an unhappy coincidence, Paul . . ."

"Paul? How does he come into it?"

"His story, Tommy. That wonderful story. Naturally it wasn't his fault, but it was a bad time to be inspired. It was too much for Clément. He became terribly—"

"Jealous?"

She turned, looking almost suspiciously at me.

"Jealous, yes, I believe that's the right word . . . Add to that the fact that Paul wasn't exactly tactful about his success, at least not if you put yourself in Clément's shoes . . . Anyway, we're all caught up in this crazy business now, and Clément won't turn back."

"But why, for God's sake?"

"Because he hasn't yet found what he's hunting for so desperately—his damned 'report from hell.' He hasn't found the raw material yet. I didn't want to believe that, but back when you were all talking in the bookmobile I took a look at his notebook: it's blank, Tommy! And this evening—I don't know what you're going to think of me, but I had to know—I got into the pocket where he stuffed that first page, the page he ripped from the notebook. He had scratched out the few lines he had written, but I recognized our favorite passage from Aimé Césaire, you know the one:

I would rediscover the secret of great communications and great combustions. I would say storm. I would say river. I would say tornado. I would say leaf. I would say tree. I would be drenched by all rains, moistened by all dews. I would roll like frenetic blood on the slow current of the eye of words turned into mad horses into fresh children into clots into curfew . . . .

"What if we all refuse to go on?" I said after a long pause.

She seemed to stagger beneath an invisible burden. "Don't count on me. I owe him: I'll stick by him whatever happens. As for Paul, he'll match him step for step now, you know that."

No, I didn't know it. But I was determined to throw light on things she clearly wanted to keep in shadow. If I was destined to pursue this insane journey to the bitter end in the fantasies of my three friends, I might as well do it with full knowledge of the facts.

Nathalie left me without saying another word. When I got back to camp I was too upset to sleep. I lay there trying to disentangle the skein of speculations filling my thoughts. The heat was as oppressive as ever. Even night had brought no respite. There was no breeze to waft in the odors of the shore. I felt as if the heat all around us might turn into a sea of dead sand and bury us.

Little by little a dense silence stilled the noises of the night. The darkness vibrated. A supernatural wave rolled over and drowned the sounds of life. I sat up, every sense alert. The same tremulous calm had preceded Vietcong attacks in the old days. This reminder of a hated past triggered a curiously ambivalent reaction in me, a reaction that was not entirely negative.

As I sat up, the silence became even more dense: a noiseless, vertiginous buzzing. Beings and things hovered petrified in expectation of what was to come. Then, somewhere ahead of me, at a distance I couldn't gauge, there was a crackling — low at first, then louder and louder — rising skyward from the depths of the bush, swelling steadily until it filled the whole horizon and began to advance toward me.

★ *15* ★

Paul and Nathalie woke with a start. Clément went on snoring behind his hood, probably anesthetized by all the rum he had put away since our paths and the teachers' had crossed.

The crackling was racing in our direction. At first I thought it was automatic fire, but that was impossible: the noise would have been accompanied by flashes; it would have been more intermittent, broken by intervals of silence; we would have seen tracers.

Suddenly I recognized it: what was rushing toward us at the speed of a galloping horse was simply rain — the rain the island had been awaiting for so long — as if it were trying to make up for its lateness by its extreme violence. Tepid, heavy, noisy, the first huge drops broke on our faces, followed instantly by shafts of water that transfixed us like showers of arrows.

Clément kicked off his blankets. Soaked to the skin, we scurried to the slender thread of blue smoke that, for a few short moments, marked the death throes of our fire. There was no escaping the deluge. Our clothing already lay about on the ground in saturated heaps.

Through the hammering of the rain the echoes of a wild chant reached us, underscored by the throbbing of a heart that had nothing human about it. From the direction of Sansoupir a faint light flickered through the blackness. Like the downpour a moment earlier, it was moving toward us. Sheets of rain allowed us only glimpses of the feeble glow, sometimes washing it entirely from view, sometimes ringing it with a yellowish halo. At the heart of this vision a song was born. Five tirelessly repeated notes linked by a complex network of rhythms.

Brighter and brighter, the tinted haze kept disintegrating and taking shape again. A reddish glow appeared at its base, a coppery line that the downpour could no longer obscure. Finally, twenty yards away, human shapes loomed. The rain had plastered their long purple cotton dresses to their bodies, the material darkening on contact with their skin. In my mind I saw again the Black woman I had glimpsed a few hours earlier, trying to hide behind one of the huts in Sansoupir.

There must have been a hundred of them from villages all over the area. They were on us in a second, but they paid us no more attention than if we had been invisible. The ones in front wore wooden face masks, plastered with lime and covered with geometric decorations the color of dried blood.

Then came musicians and singers, their faces bare but liberally streaked with violent colors that had melted and run together in the rain, making their flesh look as if it were rotting. There was a holy ecstasy in their eyes, and I noticed an abnormal dilation of the pupils of those who brushed close by me.

They were beating time with short mallets on hollowed out wooden cylinders with a wide slit down their length, glistening with rain. Raw leather thongs around their necks supported these crude drums, which varied in size from a single cylinder to four lashed together.

Other men sang with closed mouths (or if they were open, their teeth seemed clenched on a chant that never faltered and never varied). They rattled calabashes, gourds filled with gravel or dried seeds, metal castanets, gutted oilcans, or animal jaws whose teeth clicked in their sockets.

Behind them surged an anonymous mass of people without masks, paint, or ceremonial robes, leaping, bounding, bobbing, throwing their arms in the air and jerking and twisting from side to side as if attached to live electric wires. Some brandished noiseless rattles woven from straw. Most carried hurricane lanterns, which explained the feeble glow we had seen trembling in the west after the storm broke.

The rain was still lashing us, but we no longer even thought of seeking shelter. We were hypnotized by the scene.

They crowded into the arena, where the waterlogged ground was already a swamp, and began to dance. The percussion instruments were now beating a pattern picked up by echoing voices. To the rhythm of this haunting phrase, several men broke from the crowd: rocking and swaying disjointedly, each approached one of the stakes bordering the great circle. They held grayish objects I was unable to identify until they set them down at the foot of the stakes.

They were animal skulls (most bearing horns); the rain drummed on them with increased fury. Women came forward to put various offerings between the gaping jaws: vegetables, fruit, cakes, brightly colored rags, unidentifiable bits and pieces. Other women followed and emptied the contents of hollowed-out coconuts on these totems.

White, brown, green, coffee-colored, the liquid streams trickled over the bleached bones and were slowly washed away, diluted, effaced by the flood that continued to pour from the skies. But the Black women kept bringing more offerings.

We were probably witnessing some fertility rite, inherited from an ancestral religion these descendants of slaves had never abandoned. They were celebrating the rains, the return of hope. Once they had made their libations they gave full vent to their joy.

The monotonous chant suddenly broke off. It was followed by an orgy of rhythms that galvanized the dancers into a series of dazzling improvisations.

## ★ *16* ★

Clément was standing next to me, his absurd hood so tightly glued to his face by the rain that it sculpted his features like a plaster cast.

As if involuntarily, he began to roll his hips and shoulders and spin round and round, violently throwing his head back, then letting it fall lifelessly forward. While the upper part of his body executed this movement, his heels stamped the ground with a sort of contained fury.

Then Clément—a man who prided himself on never setting foot on a dance floor—moved in to join the worshipers of Renewal in the arena, as if an irresistible force drew him to them. Crossing the circle of stakes to plunge in among the dark bodies, he pushed through the undulating mass to the center where the masks were bobbing.

There was a subtle change in the drumbeat, which fell back through a staccato series of adjustments to a shrill sustained throb. The natives joined hands and formed four concentric circles. They took four steps forward, then four steps back, first huddling close together, then an arm's length apart. It looked as if a giant human flower were opening and closing.

Clément had taken a place in the innermost of these circles, the circle formed by the mask-wearers. His movements were in such perfect harmony with those of his neighbors that he seemed to have taken part in these ceremonies from another world all his life.

Once again the music changed. Then our friend broke the circle, which immediately closed on him. He occupied the exact center of the arena, dancing more wildly than ever, kicking up great shoulder-high gobs of mud and leaping high into the air.

It all happened as if the other votaries in this savage cult recognized in him (perhaps because of his mask, perhaps because of his inspired dancing) a peer whose place in their community had been decreed from time immemorial. They showed neither surprise nor amusement nor anger. They accepted this unknown White man because Clément Calderanz, like them, was paying unrestrained homage to the earth's primordial rhythms. Arching his whole body in a final spasm, our friend raised his hands to his throat. As if finally setting himself free, he tore off his mask, exposing to the light of the lanterns a face aflame with an intoxication that was almost ethereal. This gesture too was an act of rebirth: a fertilization of the self through a repudiation of subterfuge.

I recalled some of the phrases spoken over the past few weeks by this man I was barely beginning to know: "We always believe in too few things . . . lack of possession . . . close the book on all that and commit himself to a new direction . . ."

If I had not been a victim of the mania common to so many novelists — that of rejecting their intelligence and the evidence of their senses in favor of intuitions of obscure origin (which they obey only if these signs seem sufficiently enigmatic, like the oracles of old) — if I had been less preoccupied with my own fate and its possible effect on my literary output, I would have discovered for myself what Nathalie had told me a few hours earlier about Clément.

He had decided that to tap the true storyteller's inspiration, he would transform his own life into a novel. An extremely naïve proposition, obviously, and laden with old-fashioned mystical overtones. But it was either that or consent to be mummified alive, paralyzed by impotence — and worse, by awareness of impotence. With the deck loaded like that, Clément was gambling all or nothing.

From the very start, though, he had run into a major obstacle: his own brilliant intelligence. The destiny of a character in a novel has to be lived firsthand. This was behind Clément's immense effort to free himself of the shackles of culture (even of civilization, with all its implied suppression of instincts, of raw desires, of ancient attitudes). In alcohol he sought a simple, swift, and tested way of shattering those barriers.

Like the barbarian he now sought to become, he had succeeded in treating us with an indifference bordering on contempt. Succeeded in behaving like a genuine bully toward Paul (whose lovingly elaborated story had been anathema to him). But he still hadn't managed to write even a single sentence of the novel for which he was ready to sacrifice his soul: to "compromise" himself, as he had put it to me one evening. To risk hellfire.

Yet his efforts had not been entirely wasted: the life force was coming alive inside him again, goading him further and further from the spurious values of his past life. Maybe he wouldn't write a book — but he himself would become a magnificent, incandescent, romantic creation.

As I stared hungrily at him — prey to a fascination that was at least as murky as Clément's motives — the masks stopped swaying; circle by circle, the whole congregation followed suit. One by one the drums fell silent. Castanets, gourds, and cowbells ceased their clamor, succeeded by the spattering of the downpour on the forest leaves. The Blacks stirred uneasily. Then they began to trickle away, melting from the ring of stakes and backing without haste into the thick surrounding vegetation. Soon all we could see of them were vague reddish reflections among the branches.

Clément remained alone in the center of the arena, a figure so purely primitive that he seemed to strike fear into the very heart of savagery.

## ★ *17* ★

The next night we reached La Lanterne. As the island sank into darkness, we set up camp at the end of the last stretch of paved road in the ruins of the filling station where this story began.

In the village the last lights went out. I fell asleep, or rather I lost consciousness, exhausted after the previous night's curtailed sleep and the rigors of a day's march punctuated by a series of storms.

Torrential rains had flooded and wiped out the Trail. How could we be sure we were still on the right track? The compass just gave us general directions, which grew vaguer when the vegetation thickened as we left the swampy flatlands of the southern part of the island behind us. Our maps turned out to be based on guesswork the farther we got from St. Elizabeth. And on several occasions we had to leave what we assumed to be our route to seek shelter from the rain.

We reached La Lanterne a good two hours behind schedule. Even then, we made it only because in the last stage of our trek the Trail followed the main highway (which allowed us to keep walking after nightfall).

We would be eating our midday meal next day at the edge of Three-and-Two-Clouds. After that—the unknown: adventure pure and simple.

"You know, the kind of adventure you encounter only in books!" Clément sneered at Paul as he drained the rum bottle obtained at the general store.

Once again, Nathalie hugged herself.

From the moment we had started walking I had been looking for a chance to be alone with Paul and ask him the questions burning my lips. I found it around midafternoon.

Paul had been bringing up the rear. A backward glance told me he had disappeared.

This would not have disturbed me if I had not had the feeling that we were being followed, or at least that many eyes had accompanied our progress since we had left the stake-ringed arena. I had no tangible proof, but in Vietnam, where such intuitions could sometimes save your life, I had learned to trust my instincts. Were Colonel Paradise's minions already spying on us? Only fear of alarming my companions had deterred me from taking out my Smith and Wesson. But during our noon halt, pretending to rearrange the contents of my pack, I laid it on top of my other things.

Seeing that Paul was no longer with us, I went back to look for him without telling the others. In any case, Clément was interested only in what lay ahead, and Nathalie was sticking with Clément, her whole attitude proclaiming that her determination had not wavered.

Our footprints had sunk deep into the waterlogged ground, and I had no trouble retracing them. In a few minutes I had found our friend.

He had unhitched his gear. Seated on the trunk of a dead tree, with his wrists dangling to his ankles and his forehead resting on his knees, he looked as if he were meditating.

I saw him jump when he heard me, but he did not even glance at me until some moments had gone by. I realized that I was looking at an exhausted man.

As I approached I noticed a detail I had missed before: Paul had taken off his boots; between the heel and the Achilles tendon both feet were bloody. Luckily I was carrying the first-aid kit.

I began to clean and dress his wounds at once. We hadn't exchanged a single word. I concentrated on the gestures that had been drummed into me, a world away from here, by a determination to live that had seemed as out of place then as a thirst for champagne on the steps of the scaffold. At the same time I congratulated myself on my foresight with all the smugness of a boy scout.

"Paul," I said, when I was through, "you're not cut out for this sort of thing."

I hadn't expected such a violent reaction. He jumped. His hand opened and gripped one of my wrists. His eyes bored into mine as though searching out hostile intentions. "Did he send you?" he ground out through clenched teeth.

I had to muster all my tact to calm him down.

"I'm here, aren't I?" was his next remark. He was blinking rapidly.

I could have sworn he was fighting back tears. I would have given a lot not to have witnessed this.

He sighed wearily and shook his head. "He's not going to get me that easily, Tommy. Oh sure, he has more stamina than I do. He's made all the rules, the way he always does, and the odds are stacked in his favor, the way they always are. But he's made one big mistake. The arsonist has underestimated the violence of his fire. In fact, I'm only beginning to realize how violent—"

I waited for him to go on. I was determined not to open my mouth until he asked me to.

"Our beloved Clément Calderanz," he said darkly and bitterly. "We all owe him so much! You feel that too, don't you? I do, Tom. I've felt it for a long time. To tell the truth, I was obsessed with it . . ."

He sighed again. "You know, I was even beginning to wonder if it wasn't Clément who was quietly buying up all the books I was supposed to be selling . . . And then one evening—one of those evenings when he seemed to be in the dumps—I played my big gratitude scene for him, hoping to raise his spirits. We were alone in the apartment (you were working at home and Nathalie was out visiting someone), and I took the opportunity to unload everything. I had to, sooner or later. Anyway, to make a long story short, I told him, 'Dear old Clément, you've taught me everything I know; if it hadn't been for you not only would I have remained unpublished but I would also have been a Sunday writer for the rest of my life.' It was the truth, wasn't it? And I added that nobody could ever repay a debt like that. Do you know what his answer was?"

He broke into a mirthless laugh that almost choked him. "I remember every word, Tommy. If they tried to dig it out of my skull they wouldn't be able to: they'd have to take my whole head off! Clément laughed contemptuously and sneered at me over his glass of cognac. Then he said: 'We're not above a bit of princely generosity in this business, kiddo—just as long as we know it won't do any good!' First of all I didn't want to believe what I had heard. He was joking: I smiled. Then he hurled his empty glass at the wall and yelled: 'I helped you because you're harmless, you poor sucker! Set your mind at ease. I don't consider you in my debt. I've taught you nothing: you'll never learn anything. What you've published couldn't matter less if you'd left it buried in the bottom of a drawer. And as for becoming a real writer—you haven't a prayer!'"

"Listen, Paul, I understand how you must have felt. But remember, he was dishing the same charming stuff out to me around that time."

"No, Tom. I know what he really thinks of you. We all do. No, you're wrong. And anyway, that wasn't all. He hadn't finished speaking his piece that night. He went on needling me. And suddenly I understood. I was staggered, but there it was: he couldn't forgive me the success of my last novel. He quite simply couldn't take it."

"Clément? Come on! It doesn't make sense."

"I'm not making it up. With the help of the booze he became more and more specific. He challenged me to try to write without his advice, without his support, without his approval— 'without a wet nurse!' he literally spat in my face. And then he shouted: 'You believe in value for money, kiddo? Then get it into your head that you're not up to challenging Clément Calderanz!' His damned crisis was nothing more than a fit of jealous pique."

It seemed impossible. Yet Paul's emphatic tones left no doubt he was sincere.

"I could have killed him," he went on. "I told him that if we ever met man to man he would crack first. I told him a whole bunch of things I wouldn't have dreamed of a moment earlier, but that I firmly believe now—that he would have to abdicate, because basically he was just a talker, and talk was the last refuge of writers without genius."

"But the crisis is over, Paul," I forced myself to object. "You accepted his invitation to come here. That means you've forgiven him."

He stiffened. "I'm not here because of Calderanz," he said. "I told him I would accept his challenge," he went on, impervious to the contradiction, "and that's what I've done!"

He had stood up and was holding his clenched fists head-high. But as he caught my eye he realized how theatrical the gesture was and immediately caught himself.

"Anyhow," he muttered, "you've already seen what a sore loser he is."

"And now?" I asked.

"Now we're not talking literature anymore. What's more, we never really were . . ."

I saw he did not want to say any more.

"Let's go," he said, hoisting his pack onto his shoulders. "We've wasted enough time already."

## ★ *18* ★

That night again something roused me from sleep. Not a sense of danger, like the night before, but a vague fear all the same, a sort of alarm without any logical cause.

In fact, everything seemed normal. Not far from me I could hear Clément's breathing, heavy with rum. Only when my eyes grew accustomed to the dark did I realize that Nathalie was not there. Her sleeping bag was a flat lifeless rectangle on the ground.

Not sure why I did what I did, I went into the next room. Paul too was missing.

I picked up my revolver and flashlight. Making sure Clément was still sleeping, I crept out of the gas station. Listening hard, scanning the darkness, I moved out to the pump.

Nothing.

I crossed the road, swinging the flashlight beam, and finally found footprints. Recent ones, obviously, otherwise the last storm would have obliterated them. They led toward the dilapidated entrance gate of the former plantation.

Beyond that point the vegetation was so tangled you couldn't see the ground at all. From there on I had to go on instinct alone. And on common sense.

A series of rocky steps to my left offered the only visible break in the jungle screen, so I took that opening. The passage led to a kind of tunnel, a narrow corridor roofed over with vines and low branches, where I had to stoop to move forward. The sky gradually vanished from sight. I had to fight the feeling that the tunnel was closing behind me with every step I took.

The tunnel veered right, abruptly widened, then stopped. I found myself back in the open air surrounded by the scents of unknown, waist-high plants. I switched off the flashlight. The clouds that had veiled the moon were dispersing. Down a slope, outlined in a bluish light at the very bottom of a deep hollow, I could just make out what remained of the plantation buildings. The atmosphere was heavy with that very special feeling that hovers over the scenes of old tragedies (Pompeii, St. Pierre in Martinique) and dead splendors (the palace of Knossos or the pyramids of Teotihuacán).

I took the gently sloping path down to the ruins. The moon — now completely free of the clouds — bathed the area in a milky light.

Only the front columns were left of what must have been the planter's mansion. They stood out in stark relief from the rest of the ruins, like a regret, or like a posthumous challenge from the vain presumptions these buildings had once stood for: an idolatrous dream, arrogantly transcribed in stone, of a civilization that had unwittingly sacrificed its most precious substance to the fantasies of grocers and accountants. Here, through a succession of compromises and retreats, the loftiest speculations of Greece had ended . . .

I froze. Nathalie and Paul were silhouetted between two columns, thirty paces from where I stood. They were facing one another, barely a yard apart. I realized from their positions that they were conversing in low voices, even though no words reached me.

Why was I here? I had stuck my nose into something that was no business of mine, even though I was piously shocked by what I had just found. What should I do now? Let them know I was here? Since I had heard nothing of what they were saying, this seemed excessively delicate; it might simply confuse them, without atoning for my indiscretion at all.

I was about to withdraw, feeling very angry with myself, when I saw something that finally and completely destroyed me. The woman's head tilted sideways and backward, approaching the male profile until the two silhouettes blended in the kind of communion that left no doubt about its nature.

<h2 style="text-align:center">★ 19 ★</h2>

I had already turned my back on them and was beating a retreat as fast as I could without catching their attention. I fled in the crazy hope that every step I took would cancel out a step I had taken in the other direction.

What a damned idiot I had been! I hadn't grasped a single one of Paul's hints, although they now seemed crystal clear. As for Nathalie, if I had admired her discretion simply because she had not shown her feelings to me, was that any fault of hers?

No, I was the cause of my own bitterness. Right from the start, I had been interested only in myself. I had been clinging to the illusion that I had bravely renounced Nathalie after that melancholy afternoon in the Luxembourg Gardens. Was my chivalrous heart now going to wallow in self-pity because someone else had been less scrupulous than I had been? Or rather, less hypocritical. And more successful.

When I emerged from the vine tunnel near the monumental

entrance to the plantation, the sky was once more covered with a layer of clouds so low they seemed to be touching the treetops.

Reaching the gas station, I began to tiptoe so as not to waken Clément. I need not have bothered: the station was deserted. The hood lay in the middle of the room, a shapeless lump.

I went out again to look around the ruined station. As I was finishing my inspection, which yielded no results, I heard a mocking voice behind me: "Well, Tom, bringing me your report?"

Calderanz emerged from behind a thick bush, a smile on his lips. A cold glint by his knee drew my eyes to the revolver hanging at the end of his arm, as if he had forgotten its existence.

"That's what you meant to do, wasn't it, old friend?" he went on with heavy sarcasm. "You had some fascinating things to tell me? And so touching, no?"

I said nothing.

"You disappoint me, Tommy," he said. He sounded like a man amused by a piquant state of affairs. "And here I was thinking you were my best friend."

He burst into a ringing laugh. I merely looked steadily into his eyes.

He shook his head. "Don't worry. I'm kidding. Don't I have the right to some fun too?"

"Who else is having fun?" I said, more coldly than I really intended.

"True. You're right as usual . . . Thank heaven, none of this is a game. We've finally left childhood behind us . . ." (He briefly raised the hand carrying the weapon.) "This revolver is loaded, after all. Oh, don't be alarmed: I have no intention of using it. Not tonight. I'm not going to use it on you, or on me, or on them—I mean *him*. Let's just say that the indisputably material nature of this article proves that we are well and truly in the real. You understand?"

"I'd rather not understand."

"But that can't be, Tommy. No, it cannot be. You're an intelligent young man . . ."

"No, I'm not, if you want to know the truth."

"Who's the most intelligent of us, would you say? I'll tell you: Nathalie."

A look of great weariness suddenly crossed his face, reminding me of Paul a few hours earlier.

"Let's sit down," said Clément in a subdued voice. "Please. Let's talk a little."

I obeyed. He sat heavily beside me.

"You know, Tommy," he began, "she should have left me. You can't imagine the tortures I put her through those last months in Paris . . . I'm not trying to excuse myself. You were there: you came in for your share. But it was nothing compared to what she had to go through. I had lost a lot more than the power to write; or rather — it amounts to the same thing — the power to read my writings without getting sick to my stomach. Listen, Tommy. Listen to what I'm telling you: I was a sick man. Do you understand? And he, he was strutting around as if no illness could touch him! To use the half-baked terms he's so fond of, I no longer deserved Nathalie, and he realized it. I was getting a little weaker every day, and that girl is strong, old man, terribly strong. She truly 'deserves' to be loved. I mean, the only way to love her is to deserve her love. And believe me, that's no small order! No ten-cent shading of blues will do the trick! What an ass, to think he could pull it off so cheaply. Oh, Tommy, don't ever let anyone tell you they owe you everything: they'll never forgive you for it. And they'll be ready to kill for a song about a bench covered with snow . . . The tiniest compliment from a woman and they'll think they have the power of life and death over all creation."

"If you're talking about Paul, he didn't give me that impression the night he read us his story."

"Good old Tom! You didn't see what I saw. But it doesn't matter. Believe me, I'm grateful to him for weaving that vaporous twaddle, and even for trying to exploit it as shamelessly as he did. It opened my eyes. It freed me; yes, it freed me. It taught me that writing was the exact opposite of that kind of needlepoint. That the superiority I had come within a hair of granting him turned out to be bluff pure and simple! Hot air, Tommy! Sand in the eyes! I behaved like a swine, a swine and a certifiable idiot, but I swear that's all over now. I'm going to win her back, old man, that's what I'm going to do. I've found my path. It took some time, I admit, but at long last I know where to look for the Promised Land. Him I don't give a damn about. But Tommy, wait until you read my next book!"

"You mean your report from hell?"

"What else? I'm going great guns, Tom. It's never gone better: it's as if the damn thing were writing itself!"

He didn't even blink; I was the one who had to look away.

"If Paul doesn't matter," I said to cover my embarrassment, "why put him through an ordeal that's beyond his strength? What are you trying to prove, and to whom?"

"He's here, isn't he?" he burst out. "He says so, often enough! He's here, and he's one too many — the way he always is. Remember what I told you the first time we discussed him?"

I remembered: "Why do people want to become writers? Why aren't you and I the last surviving representatives of the species on earth?"

"You're the one who imposed him on us," I said gently.

"Imposing someone worthless on others, when one can't even impose oneself on oneself, is a kind of consolation." He muttered the words without much conviction, it seemed to me, then stood up, ending the conversation.

I followed him back inside the station, and we stretched out in our sleeping bags. Clément had put his mask back on. Was he really asleep again or was he — like me — waiting for our companions to return?

Nathalie appeared first. She slipped into the room without a sound: Clément's chest continued to rise and fall with perfect regularity. A few minutes later I heard Paul's stealthy movements in the next room: still Clément did not react. How did he manage to create such a void inside himself after such emotional turmoil? I knew I wouldn't be able to sleep until exhaustion forced me.

The sky started to grumble again. There was a fresh storm of exceptional violence. I tried in vain to focus on the natural phenomena that came with it. I winced mentally at the memory of Clément's pathetic lie about his writing. As pathetic as his blindness to what was happening between Paul and Nathalie.

Win her back? It was a little late for that. If Paul was one too many, obviously all of us didn't think so.

What I found hardest to accept was Nathalie's betrayal of a man she knew would forgive her no matter what she did. Her shabby behavior contradicted the image I had had of her ever since we first met. She was the last person in the world I would have expected to sink below her own standards.

A second storm blew up, driving away the memory of the first. Then, around four in the morning, there was a gunshot, perhaps a hundred yards from the camp. I sprinted outside with my gun and flashlight, closely followed by the three others. Never had a deeper calm, a more voluptuous peace seemed to reign over the island.

★ *20* ★

It wasn't our last surprise. It soon became apparent that Father Van Doren had played on our gullibility. About the mosquitoes, for example. They were no more plentiful around Three-and-Two-Clouds than they had been in the rooms of the Christophe-Liberté. The baneful influence of the armed gangs? Except for its topography, the north was not visibly different from what we had seen of the rest of the island. The natives' behavior was the same here as everywhere else, an indefinable blend of shyness and hostility, openness and mistrust, indifference and curiosity. As far as their feelings toward us were concerned, their crazy reactions hinted at everything and the opposite of everything. The two French teachers had also felt like victims of a cat-and-mouse game. But was it really a game? All I could say for sure was that the islanders weren't any more or less friendly, any more or less reticent and hostile beyond La Lanterne than on the St. Elizabeth side. If my Vietnam experience was anything to go by, this attitude did not square with Father Van Doren's picture of a civilian population terrorized by gangs of perverted drunkards and criminals.

Could the notorious Paradise and his cronies have withdrawn to the far northern tip of the island? There seemed little reason for scum like that to limit their activities if government indifference guaranteed them immunity. Unless the villagers' seeming passivity meant they had nothing to fear from the bandits — in other words, that they were in cahoots with them.

Clément must have been thinking along the same lines, for he asked the first Black we met along the Trail if there was any chance of our meeting Colonel Paradise before nightfall. But he was not wearing his mask, and the man's only answer was to bolt into the brush at top speed.

To stop my companions from worrying about this incident, I told them I would ask a few discreet questions when I went to the store at Three-and-Two-Clouds to buy supplies. I felt in total control of myself. My only worry stemmed from this serenity, in fact. Could I be nostalgic, somewhere deep in my heart, for combat, for hazardous missions? Perhaps only Thelonious Monk could have answered me. I missed his music. And the blindfolded reader at the bottom of my pocket was not the kind of idol you would entrust with your fate.

After what had happened the previous night, Paul should have been showing signs of satisfaction; and Nathalie, it seemed to me, should have been feeling some embarrassment at finding herself caught between two men ready to tear each other apart over her. But that wasn't the case. Paul appeared to be sulking, while Nathalie was all serenity and self-confidence.

I had missed something important. But what? What hadn't I grasped? Was the rest of this trip going to be uncertainty and mystery? I began to think so even more as it became apparent, from the topography and from my compass readings, that Three-

and-Two-Clouds could not possibly be where the maps—however tentatively—said it should be.

At every village we passed along the Trail the inhabitants—just like those in Vietnam at the beginning of my tour of duty—were free with their smiles (some even broke into infectious hilarity) but seemed stricken by some strange malady whenever we needed simple answers to simple questions. If we persisted, they showed total incomprehension. From the way they gaped and rolled their eyes when we mentioned Three-and-Two-Clouds, you would have thought we were asking about some place on the moon in the vicinity of the Sea of Tranquility. We were experiencing that strange concept of human communication Michelle and Julien had described to us.

At the third hamlet (even more destitute than the two previous ones, and partly abandoned), the Black man I attempted to question fled even before I opened my mouth. Losing my temper, I chased after him.

Every now and then he threw backward glances at me, but so mockingly that I suspected he had deliberately taken flight in order to make me follow him. We reached the forest; suddenly he veered left and vanished as completely as a ghost.

But a moment later I heard branches crackling about twenty yards ahead, on the far side of a small cleared space where I had halted to look around. Thinking I saw a flash of brown skin among the vines, I raced forward—and sank waist-deep in liquid mud.

This time there was no mistaking malevolent intent. The trap had been carefully covered over with foliage. I let loose a string of curses that did honor to the verbal invention of the United States Marine Corps.

Meanwhile, the others had caught up with me. As soon as they saw me floundering and cursing in my mud bath they broke into uncontrollable laughter; I soon joined in. It was as if all the tensions of the Trail had snapped. As I hauled myself out of the mud they flopped down to catch their breath. Fat tears rolled down our cheeks. The moment one of us began to heave again

with silent mirth, we all rolled helplessly on the ground, grip-
ping our stomachs with both hands.

Luckily there was a stream nearby. I washed my things in it,
then stripped naked and bathed, out of sight of my friends, who
were preparing our meal fifty yards upstream. To my surprise,
the water was deliciously cool. I stayed in it longer than was
strictly necessary to get cleaned up.

That moment of shared laughter made me think back with
regret to our evenings in Paris before Clément had begun to
doubt himself. I wondered if we would ever again find enough
wisdom within ourselves to reject the fascination of savagery, to
return to that existence, which — in both its lighter and its deeper
moments — represented a conquest of the mind. The civilization
we were breaking away from certainly had its share of weak-
nesses, flaws, and corruption — but *it was ours,* and what Clément
chose to see as a challenge was probably nothing more than an
escape.

When I rummaged through my pack for clean underwear, I
was shocked to find that my maps had disappeared. Likewise, no
matter how hard I looked, I couldn't find the compass I had put
down on a large rock before bathing.

At first I attributed this new trick to the islanders' passion for
unpleasant jokes. But the more I thought about it, the likelier it
seemed that Paul and Clément both had stronger motives for the
theft. Clément because it would have been a way of adding spice
to our adventure; Paul because it might force cancellation of the
expedition before he himself had to call it quits.

When I reported my loss to them, both reacted like perfect
suspects, almost as if they had rehearsed their reaction
beforehand. Paul declared that it would be ridiculous to carry on
under the circumstances. Clément retorted that, on the contrary,
he considered the incident an added reason for forging ahead.

"This isn't a guided tour!" he exclaimed. "How boring it
would be without risks or suspense. We might as well play
cowboys and Indians in the schoolyard and shoot each other
down with our index fingers!"

And then, since I clearly wasn't showing enough enthusiasm to suit him, he added: "Surely you agree, Tommy? Otherwise why would you have risked catching schistosomiasis just for the pleasure of a cool bath?"

I had forgotten about schistosomiasis, the disease transmitted by microscopic worms common in Caribbean streams (if they can manage to get under your skin). Clément hadn't forgotten, but he had elected to let me go ahead — presumably, to add another dramatic touch to our scenario. That kind of dedication could land us all in an early grave.

"Tell me something, Clément," my other friend exploded. "Why don't you just empty your gun into us? That would save time, wouldn't it? And then you would be certain of being the greatest writer on the island. Then you wouldn't even have to pretend to be scribbling in your little notebook."

Before I could even move, Nathalie was shielding Paul with her body.

"Paul's at the end of his tether," she said briskly and firmly. "With those sores, every step must be torture for him."

None of us seemed to know where she was heading, but strangely enough Paul appeared even more confused than the rest of us.

"I'll make it," he protested. But his voice betrayed the effort it took to convince himself. Nathalie's statement, however dispassionately delivered, seemed to have snapped a spring inside him.

She turned to look at him. "You don't have to prove anything to anyone, Paul. We all know you're in no shape to go on. What's keeping you here?"

The cynicism of her question staggered me.

Paul stared at the ground between his feet. "And all of you, what's keeping you?" he muttered in such wretched tones that I believed he was going to cry.

"Clément has to finish what he's begun," she answered somewhat stiffly.

He rocked his head heavily from left to right. "What has he begun?"

"Listen, pal," said Clément, for once conciliatory, "you don't have to worry about all that."

Paul clasped his temples in his hands. "I'm here, aren't I?" he sighed.

A moment later it started to rain again.

★ 21 ★

The afternoon was nearly over when an old islander, one of a group toiling in a scrubby sugarcane patch, kindly let me know (as if he were giving me the most commonplace information) that Three-and-Two-Clouds was a few miles behind us.

From his description I recognized the destitute village where I had chased one of his fellow islanders. "Is this the region they call the Mirror Swamp?" I asked.

He stretched an arm to the west. "Mirror Swamp," he said with a leer that exposed bare, bleeding gums.

My companions had stopped short about twenty feet away, the way they always did when I needed to parlay with the natives. So I was surprised to hear Clément's voice boom out behind me. "And Concession Eighteen? Are we far from Concession Eighteen?"

But naturally, as soon as he saw Clément, the peasant shut up like a clam and turned on his heel. We had just discouraged our first willing informant since La Lanterne. Another was not likely to turn up soon.

"Oh well," Clément snickered, "if that's their game, I'm not worried. We still have a few cards up our sleeves, don't we, Tom?"

He took his holster from his pack and slung it on his hip. To my astonishment, Nathalie immediately followed his example. Where was the diffident girl with whom I had strolled through the Luxembourg Gardens? Or the girl who had implored my help two evenings ago? And who, the next night, had given Paul that Hollywood-movie kiss in the kitschy moonlit setting of the ruined plantation?

"That girl is strong, old man . . . The only way to love her is to deserve her love . . ." Clément's words rang in my ears like a sad, bitter Thelonious Monk tune. I certainly didn't deserve her love — not while she was the Nathalie I desired in silence, the softly luminous young woman whose hand I hadn't dared to take in the park.

The unknown woman who now stood in her place, masked by the hard glint that had entered her eyes, didn't have the power to arouse adolescent emotions in me, to revive old yearnings that I knew were ridiculous but that I prized more than anything else in the world. But I hadn't lost everything in the exchange. Because this new Nathalie was a woman I could contemplate without inhibition. Without guilt and without shame. A woman I felt entitled to make love to if the opportunity arose. A woman I would have the courage to desire passionately, rather than love.

When my maps disappeared all hope of following the Slave Trail went with them. The horizon was darkening by the time we reached the crest of a low hill and gazed out over a vast stretch of stunted scrub, framed in the distance by the rolling waves of the Caribbean: "a more credulous sea and haunted by invisible departures, like a sky tiered above orchards . . . ." But the orchards we looked upon were not those described by St. John Perse: they looked more like portals to pain and solitude; the few fruit we found there exuded filth and venom.

We resigned ourselves to making a halt on this crest. We ate our supper without uttering a word; rain interrupted the meal twice. I had to rekindle the fire. That evening Clément did not touch his bottle of rum. Then, under shifting clouds that were darker than the night, our revolvers strapped to our hips, we sought the oblivion rendered so inadequately by the word *sleep*.

Suddenly I sat up to make sure that I had not lost the figurine in my pocket while I was cleaning my clothes by the stream. No, it was still there. I let out a sigh of relief that emptied my lungs. Without worrying about my companions this time, I raised the statuette to my eyes to examine it at leisure. Was it friend or foe? Good luck charm or evil talisman?

A short while later the idea for a story suddenly came into my head.

★ 22 ★

We all slept longer than we intended, even Clément, who was usually up and chafing at first light.

Behind us, to the east, the sun had broken clear of a line of low hills. But it was still low enough in the sky to streak the landscape to our west with its long slanting rays. If that really was the Mirror Swamp stretching away to the coast, it deserved its name: it was like a vast copper plate set down on the plain and flattening every contour. A glittering plate in which I wouldn't have been surprised to see the clouds reflected.

Somewhere halfway between us and the coast, an unidentifiable object was glittering with a more brilliant light than the rest of the plain, as if someone were signaling us. It was bright as a star; and since we had no idea where or how to continue our march, it seemed natural to home in on this distant landmark, the only one we saw. I imagine too that its symbolic aspect exercised a magnetic attraction as our mood became more and more receptive to portents and myths.

Getting to the source of this light took us over four hours, although appearances had misled us to expect a shorter hike. We had to make several detours, during which the silvery light of our beacon vanished. There were downpours that utterly wiped it from sight (once for more than twenty minutes). And each time it was a source of wonder to discover our resplendent star again, not always in the spot where our eyes sought it. From certain angles it was reduced to a mere luminous point of almost unbearable intensity.

To hold it in view we tried to keep the sun at our backs, but, as I mentioned, the lay of the land often made this impossible. Meanwhile, its exact location became harder to pinpoint as the sun rose in the sky. It was as if our goal were shrinking from us the nearer we came to it.

And then, suddenly, barely two hundred yards from the small rise we had just climbed, a familiar form took shape around the point of light: the outlines of a motor vehicle parked in the middle of nowhere, far from any navigable highway. The mystery was solved: the signal we had instinctively obeyed came from the reflection of the sun's rays on its windows, rearview mirror, and chrome fittings.

Hearts pounding, we pushed on and soon recognized the bookmobile. Clément raced past me. Ten yards or so from the vehicle he stopped dead. When he looked back, I saw that the blood had drained from his face.

"Good God!" he said hoarsely. "Look at that!"

The doors and sliding door of the bookmobile were wide open. The steering wheel had been sawn off, the dashboard smashed in, the seats ripped out. Books littered the floor and the ground outside. Some of them had been piled up and burned: the ashes were still smoking. But these details, however arresting, were infinitely less horrible than the blood spattered everywhere, inside the front compartment and on the sides of the van.

Going around to the front, as Paul gave way to violent nausea, I saw that the motor had been smashed to pieces with a violence approaching the frenzy of madness.

★ *23* ★

What struck me most forcibly was the deliberately ostentatious nature of the vandalism. There seemed almost too much blood, too much damage, and above all, too many books burned: generally it is fools, not illiterates, who attack books.

In other words, this auto-da-fe was meant to hold more meaning for us than for those who committed it. It was a dizzying thought . . . It was hideous to think that the young couple might have been sacrificed merely as a demonstration. That all this, in other words, was just a spectacular warning from Colonel Paradise to those who might be tempted to violate his territory.

The spasms shaking him had forced Paul to his knees. Nathalie stood as if turned to stone, her back to the van, staring fixedly at the brush. Clément and I began to search the under-growth for bodies. There was no lack of clues. Here again, we were confronted with a profusion of indicators. From what we could read on the ground and in the trees, twenty bodies could easily have been dragged in dozens of directions. But although we found more tracks and prints than we wanted, we were unable to unearth a single article, a single piece of clothing, any kind of debris. Whatever else, we could be certain that after being butchered the two teachers had been neither buried nor left for beasts of prey anywhere in a radius of two or three hundred yards around their vehicle. I had some experience in this kind of thing, and Clément searched hard and carefully.

In fact, he threw himself into this uninspiring search with a zeal, an enthusiasm — an excitement, to be honest about it — that deeply shocked me. Within a few minutes of our grisly discovery, his horror had been replaced by a cheerfulness so out of place it struck me as obscene. I could have sworn he was congratulating himself on his good luck.

I realized I was beginning to hate him. At that moment I passionately wanted his defeat. I wanted to see the sacrilegious light flaming in his eyes snuffed out. With a resentment that was all the more fierce because it was so belated, I rebelled against his past mockery, his past insults, the intolerable arrogance with which he had once contemplated my work. The memory of his condescension and his acts of generosity made me grit my teeth. Yes, this man had humiliated me: I suddenly felt murderous as I watched his fevered face, observed the indecent, illicit pleasure he was so shamelessly wallowing in.

I hated him for it. And I hated him even more because his barbaric emotions found an echo deep inside me that I couldn't silence. I hated him because we had grown too much alike.

He had awakened in me the ancient curse of the race, all the Gothic drives: the drunken joy of carnage, the love of blood and smoke. In a few days he had shattered the veneer of breeding, the armor of principle and custom I had reconstructed with such pain after so many years. How could I ever forgive him this outrage?

And now Thelonious Monk was dying all over again. Where I was going his compelling, sublimely clumsy fingertips would be of no help to me. For I was no longer an unbelieving mercenary on a tainted crusade: this time I had a goal—to shatter Clément Calderanz's pride.

As a result, Paul's presence was now an embarrassment to me too. We had finally left the world of "fugitive gleams and muted murmurs" for the least familiar yet most primitive reality of all: the licentious reality of war. That world was closed to him. People like him enter it only as victims.

"How are your feet?" I asked with feigned concern. By reminding him of the discomfort that lay ahead, I might be able to discourage him . . . But he brushed past me with his hobbling gait as if I had become invisible.

Two hours later—dragged along by Calderanz who seemed to be obeying some mighty inner impulse—we reached an area near the coast. Above the monotonous swishing of our progress through chest-high, sharp-edged grasses, we could hear the waves breaking and lapping gently on the shore.

As long as we had been walking in open swamp country, we hadn't sensed a single human presence around us. In fact, without superhuman tracking skills, no one would have been able to follow us without giving away his position. But as soon as we pushed into the tall grass, signs of life proliferated. To our right, to our left, behind, and ahead. Sometimes it was just a furtive and mysterious trembling of the tops of the grass stalks, suddenly stopping and beginning again a little farther ahead or a hundred yards off. In theory, it could easily have been animals,

but I don't believe any of us gave this possibility a second's
thought.

In fact, at one point I thought I heard a stifled laugh. A little
later there was a shout, too brief for us to locate; and just after
that two shots cracked out. We flung ourselves to the ground in a
reflex move that earned us multiple bruises on our hands and
arms. Only Paul remained frozen upright thirty paces behind us,
with the haggard look of a suddenly roused sleepwalker.

"On the ground! For God's sake get down!" I yelled at him.
But he went on gazing around him in bewilderment, without
moving a muscle.

Yet it was highly unlikely that anyone had fired at us, because
we hadn't heard the whistle of a shot. Unless we were the prey of
truly incompetent hunters.

I got up first, half-crouched, legs spread, revolver pointing,
held at the end of my rigid arm, my body shielded, in the
instinctive firing position. I swung rapidly from the hips, ready
to blaze away at the first suspicious shape to enter my line of
vision. But no one showed himself. In fact, I didn't even see the
wisps of smoke that should have betrayed the positions of our
hunter or hunters.

Calderanz rose like a stage devil from his pit, with a laugh
straight out of third-rate melodrama, and emptied his clip into
the air.

"Do me a favor and let me know the next place we're likely to
find ammunition," I said with cold contempt.

He merely shrugged and began to reload his weapon.

Paul had struggled out of his straps and was sitting on his pack,
his head in his hands. I went up to him slowly.

"I'm thirsty," he moaned. He repeated the words several
times, as if trying in vain to understand their meaning.

I handed him my flask. From his look, you would have
thought I'd offered him a banana.

"Rum," he said tonelessly.

The rest of the day went by without any noteworthy incident.
But now an invisible escort marched with us, usually discreet
but occasionally downright noisy, with sounds and whispers and

the noise of things accidentally brushed against or deliberately bumped. And once again Clément Calderanz led the way, handling his machete with surprising ease, with a diagonal swing that began at shoulder height and faded across the opposite knee. It was as if his body had adopted the transformations of his soul.

I didn't even consider trying to take the lead from him. He was wearing himself out clearing a path for us, while I was conserving my strength and wits by following his track. I was merely curious about what inspired him to choose one direction rather than another. Basically, I think, he was trusting to luck, having persuaded himself—he was certainly capable of it—that destiny was guiding his footsteps.

Several times I noticed that he tried to shake off our guardian angels by veering right or left. It wasn't a bad idea, I had to admit, but it didn't work: every time he tried it we came up against natural obstacles that forced us to backtrack.

The obstacles were usually unsavory stretches of bog, suspiciously calm ponds, or low-lying lagoons whose muddy banks held the sinister promise of quicksand.

The landscape had changed again. The sharp-edged grass and gorse of the plain had given way to mangroves, tree formations unknown in temperate climates. Raised up on the tips of their bare roots, which sank deep beneath the surface in a tangle of knotted arches, they looked as if they were walking on water. I had seen these stilt trees before and knew that they usually had a carpet of sticky, watery mud in which it was dangerous to set foot. All we could do when we encountered them was beat a retreat back to dry land—where our shadowers patiently awaited us.

Of course, all this fruitless twisting and turning had a disastrous effect on Paul's nerves, sapping what little energy he still had. His eyes were like two pieces of dull glass.

Nathalie, on the other hand, was keeping up with her husband without any difficulty.

There had been only one downpour since daybreak. But the sky made up for its lapse in the hour before nightfall, and we had to pitch our tents in ankle-deep puddles on saturated ground. We shared a tarp to sit on during our meal but behaved as if unaware of each other's presence. Finally, I could not restrain my anger any longer.

"Clément," I said as insolently as I could, "lend me that notebook you're not using: I've had an idea for a story wandering around inside my head, and I'd like to make a few notes."

A disbelieving look came into Nathalie's eyes. Calderanz bared his teeth as if about to bite. But I will never know what he was getting ready to say, because — as if in response to my voice — something split the air between us and struck the trunk of a huge sapodilla that towered behind the campsite.

It appeared to have come from nothing and nowhere: there was no sound before it struck, and no sound broke the silence that followed its impact with the tree.

I yanked a stone axe from the trunk: it was of recent manufacture, but was a copy of the favorite weapon of the Caribs, the warlike people who had inhabited these islands before the coming of the conquistadors. I had seen several pictures of them in the books I had studied back in St. Elizabeth.

This one was meticulously carved. There seemed to be an inscription on one of its stone faces. Holding it closer to the fire, I saw that in fact it was the outline of a bird, etched into the stone in crude relief.

More excited than ever, Clément grabbed the axe from me.

"Remember, Nathalie?" he muttered in awe. "That book about Pacific animal life that someone gave us? A boring present, right? But we didn't look at anything else for a whole week. Look, look at this fine specimen of poultry! New Guinea is full of them. Know what they're called? *Birds of paradise!* The message is pretty clear, seems to me . . ."

Once again he gave his great horror-movie laugh and began to yell at the shadows around us: "Paradise, you old fraud, can you hear me? Listen to me, you great feathered asshole! This is Clément Calderanz talking to you! You're wet behind the ears, pal! You handle literary symbols like a librarian, like a nickel scribbler! Who do you think you're impressing? I haven't come all this way just to trade insults with some houseboy. Is this the best you can offer, games of hide-and-seek, you and your lousy bodyguards? Show your face! No? All right, I'll come and find you! Tomorrow! I'll teach you how to stir up strong emotions, little man, and these two amateurs here with me might learn a thing or two as well! Sleep well: you're going to have a rough day tomorrow . . ."

When he had finished he turned back to us, oozing self-satisfaction — and found himself staring into Paul's Smith and Wesson.

### ★ 24 ★

"Unbuckle that belt, Calderanz. You too, Tom. Stand next to him: I want you both in my sights. Yes, there, over there. No, closer."

His speech was jumpy, its cadence and register beyond his control. His whole body was trembling so hard I thought his teeth would begin to chatter. He made alarming sweeps with the gun barrel to stress his words. It wouldn't be too hard to take the gun away from him if the joke turned sour, I thought.

In the meantime — unlike Clément, who was foaming with impotent rage — I was enjoying this new and dramatic turn of events. I only hoped the sequel would be up to the beginning.

"You won't be going anywhere! Nobody's going! It's over!" Paul squealed, his voice threatening to betray him at any second. "There's no more trek, no more Trail, no more anything! You lose, Calderanz. You lose because you're crazy. Why not admit it? What are you waiting for? For us to be bled white by this cutthroat colonel? Is that what you're after? Ah, if only I could be sure that you would die first, I swear I'd follow you on my knees so as not to miss it! I'd crawl on my belly if I had to! Because you've made me as crazy as you. If that's what you wanted, you got it!"

Tears glittered on his eyelids. He stamped heavily in the mud, almost choking with rage. There was something pathetic about these childish gestures. I no longer found the situation amusing. I tried to catch his eye so he wouldn't notice what was going on behind him.

Clément, watching the same thing I was, could not hold back a snicker.

"There's nothing to laugh at anymore, don't you understand?" Paul yelled at the top of his lungs, jerking his revolver up to a level with his rival's forehead. "The joke's over, you bastard! We're packing up and leaving! If you really want to get killed, go on your own! Take Tommy if he's crazy enough to go with you. But you're not dragging Nathalie down with you. Not her! She's already suffered enough because of you: you're not handing her over to those thugs, you damned degenerate! Never!"

He approached Clément and stuck the muzzle of the Smith and Wesson right between his eyes. "Got the picture?"

He started violently when Nathalie called softly:

"Paul?"

She had slipped up behind him without a sound and was now standing in the spot he had just left.

"Paul?" she said again in the same soft voice.

Did he have a presentiment? I saw his head shrink reflexively between his shoulders before he swung slowly around.

The revolver in the young woman's hand was steady.

"I am going with him," she said calmly. "Clément will do what he has decided to do, and I will go with him. You can lower that gun."

He staggered as if she had struck him in the face. His arm dropped slackly to his side and the Smith and Wesson slipped out of his hand, fell beside his leg, and sank right up to the chamber in the waterlogged ground.

I could not see his face, but I had no trouble imagining the amazement and distress there. His head was shaking slowly from right to left. Calderanz began to laugh, but I silenced him with a thunderous look.

Paul unclenched his hands and spread his arms in misery. "Nathalie," he stammered. "Nathalie . . ."

"Isn't that what I've always told you?"

"But—"

"Isn't that what I've always told you, Paul?"

"He'll kill you! That's what he wants . . ."

"You're wrong, Paul. You're as wrong as ever."

He burst into tears. The scene was getting hard to stomach. I bent down to pick up my belt and holster so that I could look away.

"But I love you," he sobbed. "You love me. You know you love me!"

I watched her closely as he spoke. Looking almost motherly, she tilted her head to one side.

"Not like that, Paul . . . Not the way you think."

"Remember what I said?" Clément muttered to me out of the corner of his mouth.

I didn't answer him but pretended to be busy cleaning the mud spattered on my gun.

The woman with the revolver was that unknown person, the stranger I had seen the day before, whose intentions and imperatives I had no way of fathoming. But the woman speaking in that soothing voice sounded like the Nathalie I had always known; my throat tightened at the sound.

She holstered the Smith and Wesson and carefully buttoned the flap.

"He," Paul indicated Clément with a sweep of his arm but avoided looking at him, "he is in love only with himself and his obsessions. Can't you see—"

It was all he managed to get out.

She sighed and softly placed her fingertips on his shoulder.

"Clément and I are going right on to the end. Tommy is free: I have no idea what he will decide. But you, Paul, are in no state to go on. Don't blame yourself, it's our fault. We've all been terribly clumsy, especially me. Nobody has challenged you to do anything—" (as she was saying this her eyes were warning Clément to keep quiet) "—Clément simply wanted to make you understand that your place wasn't here with us. Particularly since this morning: you must have seen that yourself. We all have our strong points. We all have our limits. You weren't made for this kind of thing, Paul, and that's all there is to it. Go back to St. Elizabeth. Wait for us at the Christophe-Liberté. Write something while you're there. Write a wonderful story for us: that's your calling . . ."

Sure, I thought to myself, but how is he going to find his way back? He couldn't count on me to guide him. I might die in the attempt, but I planned to be around when Clément Calderanz met his match.

With a firm step the young woman headed back to the shelter she shared with her spouse. Paul remained behind, whimpering that he would never be able to write another line, that he was nothing but a third-rate writer — and that she knew it better than anyone. She had hidden the truth from him, he said; she had mocked him. She had known from the start his story was worthless, he said bitterly, but she had been careful not to strip him of his illusions: it had been such an amusing sight, hadn't it, a man making himself utterly ridiculous?

Nathalie had gone into the tent without saying a word. I thought I would choke a moment later when she emerged holding my maps and compass.

Calderanz suddenly went into a wild Indian dance, sending up showers of mud and letting out piercing howls.

Nathalie went over to where Paul had fallen, his face buried in his hands.

"With these," she said quietly, "you should have no trouble."

He did not even open his hands. My heart hammered against my ribs. Clément went on leaping about as if in ecstasy.

"Take them, Paul, you'll need them."

Our dancing friend tripped and landed on his back, his four limbs waving in the air. He let out an enormous laugh. Paul still had not moved. Suddenly the whole melodramatic scene made me sick. It wasn't just Clément's clowning. This whole tragicomedy was degrading, demeaning for all of us. I couldn't take any more.

"That's it," I said to Nathalie. "He can have the maps, but give me back that compass, please."

I think I would have hit her if she had refused. I was ready to flatten all three of them. They understood it from my tone. Clément's laugh broke off. Paul raised his head to stare at me in consternation. The young woman handed me the compass without meeting my eyes.

I went into my tent, suddenly dizzy. I reached for the thermos flask in which I kept my rum.

It was broad daylight and I felt as if a vise were clamped around my temples when Nathalie shook me awake.

Paul was gone.

## ★ *25* ★

My first reaction was selfish satisfaction. Paul's departure made everything much simpler. Nathalie, Calderanz, and I could at last move on to serious matters. Not to mention Paradise, of course, who from my point of view was merely a bit player in *our* story, even though he had the power to intervene decisively in its development. I wasn't worried about him much: having it out with him wouldn't have bothered me at all.

"I didn't think he'd give up so easily," I said, examining the things Paul had left behind: the clothes he'd worn yesterday, his Smith and Wesson, three boxes of ammunition, my maps.

"Give up? You don't think this is the work of the colonel?"

There was a hint of hope in Clément's question, however hard he tried to conceal it. It seemed a terrible waste to him that our friend's disappearance might not be a part of the adventure.

"You mean a kidnapping? What a wonderful novelist you might have been," I sneered, stressing the "might."

Clément might be obsessed with his quest, but I was determined to complicate things for him if I could. However, Nathalie intervened to divert his attention.

"It rained so hard last night the tents rattled like drums; a whole parade could have gone through and we'd have heard nothing. And the rain will have wiped out any footprints. Maybe Clément is right. If Paul had left of his own free will, would he have abandoned so many essential items?"

"Then explain to me why the colonel's thugs would have turned up their noses at a brand-new revolver but taken the trouble to steal cans of food. No, Paul could very easily have decided to leave his weapon behind, in full view, the way we found it. It would have been a way of dealing himself out. He was showing us that he refused to fight and at the same time showing us he isn't a coward, since he was giving up his only means of defense."

"Then what do you make of the maps?"

"The maps are really reliable only in places where you don't need them. He knew that; I said it often enough. He probably decided to follow the coast. It's a longer hike, but all you have to do is keep the sea on your right. He could get to Vieux-Marigot by nightfall without even hurrying. From there he can probably take a country taxi directly to St. Elizabeth. Or there are always boats."

"I think you're deluding yourself," sneered Clément.

"I think," I shot back, "that that particular disease is fairly widespread in our little society."

He turned his back on me angrily.

"In any case," he growled, "it won't be long before we know where we stand. We'll be hearing from the good Colonel Paradise before very long."

But he was mistaken.

\*   \*   \*

Since the axe incident (it had clearly been thrown with no intention of hurting us), our escort seemed to have vanished into the blue. No more laughter or whispers, not a single human sound. After the night's downpour (which I, of course, had slept through), the morning was radiant. A light sea breeze, sweet-smelling and cool, gave the illusion of springtime.

In daylight, no one would have been able to sneak closer to our tents than fifty yards without being seen. Trees and undergrowth were too sparsely scattered over the featureless terrain to allow a stealthy approach.

Clément thought we would see or hear signs of the natives again as soon as the ground gave them sufficient cover to maneuver. So he headed straight for the mangroves, to give his pursuers the chance to make contact. But with no results: Paradise and his men remained elusive.

This setback dismayed our self-appointed chief tactician. As the hours went by he was first annoyed, then irritated, and finally depressed. I watched him without a word. Nothing could have made me break silence. So Calderanz had taken the lead? Fine: I would simply follow. But he was tiring so quickly that I felt like a hunter trailing a wounded animal and waiting for it to lie down and die.

After yesterday's challenge to the colonel, Calderanz felt betrayed and humiliated by the latter's failure to respond. I have no idea what kind of confrontation he had been dreaming of, but he had staked a lot on it, and now his antagonist had denied him a battle, cynically and in violation of all the rules of the game — the very game he had dragged us all into.

The spring at which Clément hoped to slake his thirst for inspiration was drying up, just as he had thought he was close to his goal. The softness of the air, the tranquil sky, the lazy flight of seabirds, everything was conspiring to taunt him. We had our maps and compass again but what good were they? We were chasing a ghost.

Around two in the afternoon, worn out, he sat down in the poisonous shade of a manchineel tree. Nathalie unpacked our food. There was hardly any left. Tomorrow morning at the latest we would have to get to a village and hope to find a store there.

None of us felt like talking. Aside from Clément's cursing, we had not exchanged two words since setting out. Our guide waved away the plate his wife offered him. He drained his last bottle of rum, pulled on his hood, and stretched out on the bare ground as if he never intended to get up again.

I hoped he would have the sense to get out from under the manchineel if it began to rain. Every traveler in these parts knows about this tree, whose sap is swollen with acid secretions. Should I have reminded him of the danger? I had no wish to see him writhing in pain from terrible burns, but the atmosphere between us was so thick that merely addressing him would have taken an effort I dreaded. After all, I reminded myself with a shrug, he had chosen of his own free will to expose himself to the perils of a stroll through this tropical greenhouse: let him face the consequences.

After a while he did fall asleep. Nathalie and I sat there nibbling at strips of beef jerky. She was sitting sideways to me, and my eyes kept being drawn to her profile. Of all the riddles I had encountered on this island, she remained the most inscrutable. And I had no idea whether this inscrutability was the product of her bizarre conduct or of my own impaired judgment. In all probability she had changed — but not as much as the eyes through which I now observed her.

Basically, this uncertainty was okay with me. If I had understood her I wouldn't have been capable of desiring her. I mean desiring her as I did now: with a purely physical hunger. But was I reading myself correctly? Was it a merely sensual itch I was feeling? Would I have been able to satisfy this whim by sleeping with another woman, for example?

Not by a long shot: my desire would just have been heightened. Would it lose some of its intensity if Nathalie again got both closer and less accessible to me, the way she'd been when we'd walked side by side down the Avenue de l'Observatoire? That too wasn't clear. Last night, behind the revolver that another woman's hand seemed to be holding, the old Nathalie had appeared to me again, proving that she had not been supplanted by the new: wasn't I just as eager to possess her as before?

But something in me rejected this. I continued to deny these primitive drives; I still didn't want to recognize them in myself. And what if my private picture of Nathalie — the picture I hugged to myself — was in fact my last hope, my only life raft? Despite the tyranny of desire, wasn't I turning out to be attached to the very values that Calderanz, the Trail, the colonel and his dark pranks were working to strip me of?

Suddenly I was afraid. Blinded by anger, giving way to the disgust I felt at my attraction to savagery, maybe I was about to sacrifice a magnificent dream to a trivial reality. But could I still hang on to the dream after all we had been through?

Nathalie turned her head. Our eyes met. I would have given all the gold in the world to know what she saw in my eyes at that exact moment. She sat quite still, staring intently at me, her face as hard and smooth, I thought, as the stone of the axe I had stroked with my fingertips a little while ago. Her eyes were telling me something, that was certain, but I did not understand their language. By tacit agreement we had been ignoring one another for the past forty-eight hours. When she'd told me the day before that I was free to go, she had absolved me of my mission. She no longer considered my cooperation essential. Then why this sudden insistence in her gaze? A suspicion crossed my mind: had she looked at Paul this way just before their tryst in the ruins?

She had kissed him; then she had withdrawn from him and taken Calderanz's side; and now . . . Was it possible that her look was an invitation? I didn't want to believe it. I was like a toy in the hands of my fantasies. All the ambiguity of the situation was in my own eyes. With my feelings in such chaos, wouldn't Nathalie's consent turn out to be the thing I feared most? Things happened very differently in the story taking shape inside my head. Yet her eyes continued to bore into mine, stubbornly reiterating their unintelligible message. I was having more and more trouble meeting their fire. Several times I was forced to swallow.

At last she rose. Staring straight ahead, she walked slowly toward a strip of rust-colored ground that led to the shore between a double line of mangroves. I was already on my feet, realizing that nothing could stop me from responding to this woman's appeal, even if it meant losing everything connecting me to a vision of life that had once been even more important to me than life itself—that intimate certainty, that sense of funda-mental rightness that swept away all petty distractions when

Thelonious Monk did his solos in "Ruby, My Dear," "Ask Me Now," "Pannonica," or "Reflections."

And so — just when I thought I might finally have overcome it — I was overcome by savagery. An instinct bubbling up from dark depths, from a time when man conjured his nocturnal terrors in frenzy. I was going to receive what I would never have been able to ask for: a decisive victory over Clément, a victory that would also seal my own defeat — I was perfectly aware of this — and forever erase the image of a woman I had loved.

After so bitter a triumph, there would be nothing left for me to do but go after the colonel myself and hope I would not come back. And here was a strange thing. In the very act of contemplating this deathblow to Clément, I felt closer to him than in the happiest days of our friendship. I understood him. I was his double, and he was mine. Together we had invented the Trail; together we had written its story.

Nathalie had gone down to the water's edge and was staring at a pale emerald sea stained with patches of faint ocher, sepia, violet, indigo. Gazing out at the Caribbean, at the old dream of seafarers, she stood upright and still, her ankles together. I too stood still.

What was happening? Why had she drawn me to this beach? She knew I had followed her. She sensed I was there. She could hear my breathing over the slap of the waves, the wind stirring the palms, and the beating of wings above our heads. She was waiting for me, yet she did not turn. She did not spread her arms. Her neck did not tilt backward, and I did not enclose her hips in my hands. The world went on without us. Its beauty ignored us. I watched this woman watching the sea. For the life of me, I could not take one step toward her.

Suddenly I saw clearly what held me back. She was standing in that position she had adopted when we first came to the island, hugging her body with her arms. It was a gesture I thought I would never see in the new Nathalie. Should I back off now? What did she want from me? I wasn't going to be the one to break the silence, that was certain. And I had nothing to say. In any case, would I have been physically capable of uttering a word?

Time slowed to the pace of the clouds moving in procession above. In the end it was Nathalie who spoke. Without moving. Almost in a whisper: "I took the compass and the maps because I wanted to be sure Paul would leave. Because he needed an extra push, perhaps. Everything else I tried had failed. What more could I do? He had to go. I hope nothing will happen to him."

"He had to go?"

She did not reply.

"You really wanted him to give up?" I persisted. Inside me a desperate voice was begging: "Tell me the truth, Nathalie. You can't lie to me *now*. *Not now!*"

"I tried everything, Tommy."

She was stabbing me in the heart.

"I saw you under the columns last night," I said, but even before the words were out I was sorry I had spoken. I lowered my gaze because, for the first time, I was more ashamed for her than for myself.

I realized from the sound of her voice that she had turned.

"You, Tommy?"

"I didn't mean to. I was worried. I went looking for you two without stopping to think. Do we really have to talk about it? I'm sorry: it was stupid of me to tell you."

"Does Clément know?"

"No," I said. "He just guessed that you were together."

For a fraction of a second our eyes met, then darted away again. It was impossible to tell which of us was more disturbed.

"It's all my fault," she sighed. "One day I'll explain."

"Why bother?"

"Please don't say that. Not you, Tom. Don't say that. One day . . ." But she broke off. There was a brief dry crackling sound from the bushes fringing the beach. Someone had stepped on a dead branch.

I listened. There was no mistake. A human being was coming toward us, avoiding the double line of mangroves where he would have been visible from a long way off. And if my intuition was anything to go by, he was not stalking us with brotherly intentions. So Paradise had not forgotten us after all.

And Clément was lying defenseless up beyond the trees.

The distance between us, and the thickness of the undergrowth, probably meant we were invisible to our stalker. I took a quick look around. There was nowhere to hide on the beach itself. The undergrowth? Our side of the path was swampy ground; with our ignorance of the terrain we might find ourselves trapped. And we had to keep in mind that this noisy native might be some kind of beater, sent out to drive us into the arms of the whole gang. In which case the best tactic would be to let him come to us, overpower him, and then backtrack the way he had come (praying to heaven that he had not really been a scout all along).

Unbuttoning my holster with one hand, I grabbed Nathalie's wrist with the other and pulled her behind me so that my body shielded hers.

The man was moving with maddening slowness. I have no idea how long we waited, but by the time he emerged from between two currant trees about twenty yards away I felt that we had been waiting for hours. I was still holding Nathalie's arm. I could feel her veins throbbing under the skin at the base of my thumb and forefinger, and each beat of her heart hit me like an electric shock.

We were standing that way as Clément Calderanz stepped into the open, his weapon trained on us.

## ★ 26 ★

So, after all these years, we stood stupidly face to face, like two gunslingers in a Western: Clément, who had embodied all the graces of the Old World for me; and I, the survivor of a low-budget apocalypse.

It was obvious from his face that he had forced his way through rough terrain solely to catch me red-handed and have a pretext for confronting me. And I accepted this absurd situation — because I too wanted to have it out with him.

But he wasn't looking at me.

"I see we're both after the same thing, Tom," he said with a hesitant smile.

I would have preferred him to open fire without all this talk. But perhaps he was afraid of hitting Nathalie. I let her wrist go and pointed to a piece of broken plank washed up on the sand a few paces to my left.

"I'm going to stand there," I said.

"Why change positions now? It's too late for that."

His gaze wavered. "The one who shoots first dies first," he went on.

And suddenly I realized I was facing a man adrift. Nothing was left of the implacable foe determined to take my life or lose his.

I hurled my weapon as far out into the waves as I could. "I'm not going to fire at you, Clément."

"Very big of you, Tommy. It's not very nice to kill people twice."

He dropped his eyes to his own revolver and stared at it so intently that I wondered whether he was thinking of killing himself.

Nathalie ran up to him. "Tommy was only trying to protect me."

"Sure. Everyone wants to protect you from me."

"Clément! Why do you only believe what's wrong?"

"Right . . . wrong . . . Yet another theme I never handled well, wouldn't you say? I really don't seem to have much going for me. You and Paul were right, Tommy: I have nothing but blank pages in my notebook. And they'll stay that way."

He looked deep into Nathalie's eyes. His furrowed, ravaged features were those of an old man. "I wanted to redeem myself, you see. I went as far as I could go, but I'm finished . . . Ask our pal here: he's more qualified than anyone else to measure the extent of the disaster. Remember what I told you, old man, that night we were camped in the filling station?"

Did I remember? His words were branded into me. "The only way to love her is to deserve her love . . . I'm going to win her back . . ." Did the fool think I had taken his place in Nathalie's heart? How could such an intelligent man be so obtuse?

"What disaster are you talking about?" cried Nathalie. "You haven't failed. I want you to succeed! I need it as much as you do."

"Yes," he murmured thoughtfully. "A woman needs a man, doesn't she?"

She jerked away and buried her face in her hands.

"What now?" he said. "Are you going to tell me you love me?"

A terrible pallor spread from her forehead to her lips. She did not speak again until a long moment had gone by. "There are many ways of loving, Clément."

"Thanks for the elegant wording," he said harshly. "Should I put that down to tact?"

"I want Clément Calderanz to write his greatest book! Don't you understand that? For that I would follow you anywhere and make any sacrifice! Don't you believe me? Is it possible you still don't believe me?"

He laughed sarcastically. "I'm willing to admit you think Clément Calderanz deserves every kindness. But the trouble is, Clément Calderanz is dead — and don't expect me to weep over his grave. He doesn't exist; what's more he never did exist. Clément Calderanz was just an illusion."

"No! Clément Calderanz is the greatest writer I know."

"It's true you have known quite a few . . ."

She shook her head as if to banish the sneer. "The greatest writer alive! And I want him to go on writing!"

"Alive? He was the opposite of alive! And he wasn't writing anymore: he was clowning."

"Clément Calderanz loved me, and I loved him."

"You loved a shadow, Nathalie. But I see now that even there I had an edge on you. I didn't lose you today. Nor the evening you went to Paul. I lost you the moment you preferred this zombie here to me."

He walked down to the water, gripped his Smith and Wesson by the barrel, and duplicated my gesture of a few minutes before, throwing the gun out into the waves.

"Even that joker Paradise has let me down!" he cackled. "It's time to put this story to bed!"

* 27 *

Back at camp we decided we would buy provisions at the next village, then return to St. Elizabeth by the shortest and safest route.

The storekeeper was an Indian. Sweating, flaccid, gloomy. Probably a descendant of the men who made the incredible journey after 1848 to replace emancipated slaves on the island's plantations.

As he put together the supplies I had requested — given his lightning-quick disposition, the task seemed likely to go on forever — I looked around the store. The first thing that struck my eye was a row of axes, lined up head to tail on a tall broad chest of unpainted wood. Stone axes, instantly recognizable by the birds of paradise on their blades — a touch of the exotic, the poetic, that softened their inherent ferocity.

The Indian noticed my interest. *"Des souvenirs,"* he called to me from the back room. *"Haches caraïbes.* Carib axes. *Pas chers.* Low price."

Obviously my American accent was stronger than I had imagined.

"Thanks a lot. *Merci beaucoup,"* I replied, falling into the same hybrid Anglo-French jargon. *"Pas besoin.* No need. I already have one of these things."

"As you like sir. *Comme vous voudrez.* These cost not much. *Presque rien.* Very very cheap."

I liked this Hindu merchant. Despite his air of deep gloom, he was totally unlike any of the islanders we had met so far.

"Too cheap for me then," I said just for the pleasure of hearing my own reply in English. *"Trop bon marché pour moi."*

He did not disappoint me. "Well, *you* sell me something! *Alors, vendez-moi quelque chose, vous,* if you're so rich!"

"What about my soul? *Que diriez-vous de mon âme?"*

*"Votre âme?* A man's soul? Too cheap for me, sir!"

I roared with laughter, and he joined in.

"Good answer! *On s'amuse bien chez vous. Je reviendrai!* I'll be back."

"I'm afraid not. *Je ne crois pas, monsieur.* Nobody come back. People are not such fools! *Les gens ne sont pas si fous!"*

He had stopped laughing, and a moment later my own mirth died. Still nosing through his shelves, I saw three rows of blindfolded reading women, identical to my own. There must have been thirty of the statuettes, buried to their knees in years of reddish, powdery sawdust.

The Indian came out of the back room with my supplies. He seemed to be intrigued at finding me in this part of the store, but this time he said nothing. A diffidence I could not explain kept me from questioning him. And I hoped I would be smart enough to leave the village without trying to clear up the mystery.

"Nice work, isn't it?" I said, forcing myself to sound casual as I pointed to the shelf. *"Joli travail."*

He was adding up my bill. He cast me the briefest glance from beneath eyebrows that glistened as if they had been polished. "Devil's work," he mumbled. *"C'est l'oeuvre du démon."*

Obviously he did not want to say any more.

"How much? *Combien?"*

"Devil needs no money, sir. *Qu'est-ce que le diable ferait de votre argent? Excusez-moi, mais elles ne sont pas à vendre.* Not for sale, sorry. I'm a superstitious old man. I am scared, you understand?"

"Scared?"

*"Est-ce qu'il vous faudra autre chose?* Anything else, sir?"

But he had not given me nearly enough.

"Why have them here then?" I began. "If—"

I was interrupted by bedlam outside. I recognized Clément's voice. I had asked him to wait with Nathalie outside the village. I didn't want the natives vanishing into thin air as soon as they set eyes on his face. Particularly because that face—since the scene on the beach—was so ravaged by weariness, disappointment, and anguish that it had become truly terrifying, even to me.

"I'll be back," I shouted to the storekeeper as I dashed outside.

Fifty yards to my left, surrounded by a group of men keeping a respectful distance and clearly uncertain of how to intervene, Clément had hold of a Black man who was howling in terror. With one hand around his neck, Clément held the man tight to his chest, the muzzle of a revolver pressed to his skull (I guessed the weapon was Nathalie's or Paul's). The young woman stood aside from the group, wringing her hands as she watched the scene. As soon as she saw me she ran up.

"Paradise!" Clément was yelling to drown out his prisoner's shouts. "Take me to Colonel Paradise!"

Whenever one of the villagers started to approach, he swung the barrel at him, forcing him back into the circle. I noticed that the natives' expressions reflected revulsion, mingled with a certain fascination, rather than rage or fear.

"He's gone crazy!" Nathalie whispered to me.

I walked forward slowly, calmly, to avoid any violent reaction.

"What's going on, Clément?" I said as carelessly as I could.

"You keep out of this!" he bellowed. "Take Nathalie to St. Elizabeth. Take each other, and I hope you explode with happiness! This is my business. Mine and the colonel's, which is where this hysterical idiot is going to take me. Aren't you, comrade?" He stroked the man's nostrils with the barrel of the gun.

I took another few steps. "That poor bastard doesn't even know what you want."

Clément laughed unpleasantly.

"What I want? That doesn't concern anyone—you or him! He just has to follow orders!"

I went a little closer, and did my best to translate Clément's demands into island-style French. Clément began to holler as soon as he heard the name of Paradise.

"Yes! Paradise! Paradise! Paradise!" he yelled, waving the Smith and Wesson over his head. "I want to go to Paradise! That's simple enough, isn't it?" (He fired two shots into the air.) "I have nothing more to ask of Nathalie," he went on in a calmer voice. "As for you, Mr. American-in-Paris, I never expected anything from you: it was the other way around, wasn't it? Whereas this dear colonel has proved his mastery in a field I want to get into. Paradise, you old rascal! There's a storyteller for you — and one who doesn't give a shit about fine phrases because he works in flesh and blood, if you'll pardon such a crude expression. You want me to miss the chance of a lesson like that? I'm going to write, old man: I'm going to write my own life! Fuck off!"

His hostage, eyes bulging, half strangled by the tight hold, was no longer struggling. His skin was turning marble gray. Half dead with fear, he managed to jabber out a few words.

"What did you say?" asked Clément angrily, not understanding a word.

And to me: "What is this bird singing?"

"It looks as if I might still be useful to you after all," I said without expression.

I wasn't going to leave him now whatever happened. And neither would Nathalie, I knew only too well. There was no point in trying to stop him physically: he had the revolver. We wouldn't avoid the tragic fate he was bringing down upon himself. Hadn't we always sensed that?

"What did he say?" Clément barked again.

The mouth of the revolver was on my chest.

"Just that he's ready to do what you want. But on condition" (this was my own invention) "that you let him breathe a little."

Reluctantly Clément relaxed his grip.

"Get moving," he growled.

Understanding nothing, the man naturally stood immobile, his legs wobbly, screwing up his eyes so that he would not have to look Clément in the face.

"I believe," I said, "that you're not ready to fire your interpreter just yet."

"This is *my* business," he grunted threateningly.

I merely shrugged. Haltingly, I tried to explain to the villagers that their friend would be returned to them safe and sound. Luckily the polyglot Indian had come out of his store and came to my rescue. I handed money around to compensate them for the inconvenience. I gave the man who had agreed to lead us to the colonel several banknotes (a fairly hefty sum, in fact, given the grinding poverty of these backcountry areas).

Even though he was boiling with impatience, Clément did not interfere. I promised the unhappy man that he would be allowed to leave as soon as he had brought us to our goal. It would take an hour to get there, he told me, provided it didn't rain. In a barely audible voice, he added something whose meaning escaped me.

I looked at the Indian, who was following the conversation.

He avoided my gaze. "He will guide you," he muttered. *"Il vous guidera.* But he wants the dead man to stay as far as possible behind him."

"He wants the dead man to stay as far as possible behind him?" I repeated in amazement. "The dead man?"

"That's the name they call your friend," he said more softly. *"C'est comme cela qu'ils appellent votre ami."*

## ★ 28 ★

Nobody followed us as we left the village. Stranger still, nobody bothered to come to meet us.

Not that I had been expecting a welcoming committee: I hadn't reached that stage of passivity yet. But I found it hard to imagine a gang leader not surrounded by spies, guards, sentries. I even began to wonder if our guide had understood our request, or if he wasn't taking us on a wild goose chase (which wouldn't have particularly bothered me either).

Around five in the afternoon the sky suddenly turned black; the next moment an inky cloud split open right overhead. It was less a downpour than a flood. For forty minutes or so we couldn't take a step. By the time it was over daylight was fading and there wasn't the slightest sign that we were anywhere near an outlaw's lair.

At that moment our guide pointed to a whitish patch far off among the trees.

"Padadise!" he said.

"Your personal Promised Land," I said for Clément's benefit, as he moved to the head of our column and began to hack away furiously with his machete.

We had gone twenty yards when I realized that the Black had given us the slip. I couldn't help thinking longingly of my Smith and Wesson, now at the bottom of the Caribbean Sea. If we were going to be ambushed, this looked like a particularly good spot.

But the only resistance we met came from the tropical under-growth. Could the colonel and his gang have taken off? Unlikely. Were they so ignorant of our intentions that they hadn't spotted us yet? Impossible: Calderanz and his chopper were making enough din to advertise our presence a mile and a half in all directions.

Then I remembered the words of the self-proclaimed Dutch priest, Van Doren, the first time he spoke to us, in the hotel dining room. According to him, the rabble infesting the north of the island were given to orgies of rum that put them out of action for long spells. Could the colonel be snoring away, surrounded by his comatose legions? Wouldn't at least one of them have remained clearheaded enough to keep watch in case of attack by a rival gang? It seemed an unlikely scenario; and a few minutes later, when the whitish patch we were approaching took on shape and outline, it seemed even more unlikely.

I could make out a mansion, built in a style going back to the early years of the last century, as far as I could judge. Wealthy settlers had lived here once. French-liveried servants in white gloves and powdered wigs had greeted their masters' guests on an immense terrace leading to a brilliantly lit reception hall: a string quartet had played softly; ladies in long flowing gowns had floated over the marble floor, slipping from group to group like sailing ships cleaving the sparkling sea at dawn.

Here luxury, proud display, and insolent ease had held court among soft whisperings of scandalous gossip. Vienna, Rome, and Paris had imposed their absurdities on these people. I recalled Alejo Carpentier's sublime descriptions in *Explosion in a Cathedral* and *The Kingdom of This World*. But that age had vanished long ago; now the tropics were savoring their revenge.

Nature had insidiously reclaimed her own. Day by day, year by year, she had crawled toward the haughty dwelling, encroaching from all sides, finally closing in on it and paralyzing it in a web of oozing vegetation. An enormous tree now thrust its thickest branch through one of the windows. Massive knotted roots heaved the terrace apart like the broken slab of an ancient tomb. Although relatively intact, the whole building looked like a cataclysm about to happen, perhaps because the unstable ground on which the foundations rested had shifted toward the nearby shore, tilting on one side and rising on the other so that the entire house was now askew, as if poised to lurch into the swamp.

An air not just of decay but of desolation hovered over the cracked corbels, the piers, the cornices, the dilapidated roof.

It was hard to imagine a gang of thugs camping within these walls. An old hermit, perhaps . . . Could the villager have been lying to us, even at the risk of having the "dead man" descend on him again? It was unlikely. But what other answer was there? Did the apparent absence of life mean that Paradise was alone in the house? Sick? Wounded? Dead? I preferred not to think of Calderanz's reaction if he found a corpse instead of the man whose secret he was pursuing.

We were now a stone's throw from the terrace. Calderanz put the machete back in its leather sheath, wiped the sweat from his forehead with his forearm, made sure his holster was buttoned down, made a megaphone of his hands, and shouted:

"Paradise! Colonel Paradise! Here I am! You know who I am . . . You know it better than I do. That's why I'm here. I want to talk to you."

There was no reply. Inside the house nothing moved.

"All I want is a chance to talk, Colonel!" he shouted again. "Then you can do what you like with me!" He turned to glare at Nathalie and me. "It's because of you. You're ruining everything! Get the hell out of here!"

But someone had just appeared, framed in the main door, and was crossing the terrace as if in slow motion. Someone looking bored and unconcerned. Someone whose skin was white and whose clothing didn't bear the slightest resemblance to a uniform. Someone who surveyed us without surprise and without pleasure. Someone we had already met: a ghost named Julien.

★ 29 ★

Calderanz staggered; Nathalie had to put a shoulder under his arm as we climbed to the head of the terrace stairs where the teacher, his hollow cheeks dotted with the early scrub of a beard, stood waiting for us.

We were still a few steps from the front door when I was caught by a smell, as faint as that of dead leaves but as heady as a whiff of venison, that grew stronger as we moved forward. Inside the main hall, the stench of a slaughterhouse assailed our nostrils.

The hall was full of long, rough-cut wooden pews stacked in the utmost disorder. Some sat on top of others; some lay on their sides or backs; some, too split or broken to serve their purpose, leaned against the walls. The remains of a small stage (barely higher than a speaker's dais) filled one end of the hall; water dripped from rust-colored patches mottling the ceiling. You had to dodge the puddles glowing in the fugitive twilight.

Michelle had spread an old piece of blanket on the only part of the stage that could still be walked on. She was lying on it, a book in her hand, in a posture that would have been appropriate in a convalescent clinic or an opium den. She did not seem surprised to see us either. But was she still capable of surprise, I wondered? Impervious to the smell of putrefaction all around her, she gazed absently at us, her eyes veiled by some mysterious daydream. She did rise to a sitting position, drawing her legs up beneath her, but so languorously that she might have been moving in a liquid environment.

Perhaps the young couple were still in shock after the attack they had suffered. But in that case where were their wounds? How had they escaped the butchery?

It was the first thing Clément asked them.

The bookmobile had broken down, they answered without further elaboration, as if the subject were of no interest. Julien hadn't been able to get it going again. They had wandered across country, carrying their most valuable books, until someone suggested they use this sumptuous mansion as a base.

Neither of them showed the slightest interest when we told them about the state in which we had found their vehicle. Julien seemed more anxious to talk about the house we were now in; one of his books had been full of exciting information about it. The islanders knew this place as "Paradise House" (which probably explained why our guide, misunderstanding our question, had led us here). At the end of the eighteenth century, the estate, run by the mansion's owners, had employed an emancipated slave as overseer: a young man of exceptional intelligence who had learned to read and write and to comment on Rousseau's writings for the entertainment of his owners (who made it a point of pride not to understand those writings), and who was said to be the only Black man in the islands to wear glasses. It was he who later gave the signal for the great rebellion and led the uprising. It was believed too that he was the man who organized the collective psychodrama in which the Whites were brought face to face with the frivolity of their customs and the emptiness of their beliefs.

For years, Captain Charles-Edmond de Barigny of the French navy, who had led the reprisals following the uprising, hunted this man up and down the island, laying cunning ambushes, offering rewards to anyone who would betray him; many years later he even offered amnesty to the renegades, simply for a chance to study this extraordinary character. All his efforts were in vain.

At the age of twenty-three, Julien went on, the ex-slave had been baptized; and, since a first name alone would have been beneath the dignity of this Black prodigy, the priest had tacked on the first surname that had come to his lips. Ever since, the ex-slave had been known as Jean Paradise.

"So it's thanks to this man," Calderanz concluded, "that there's a Colonel Paradise today."

Michelle and Julien exchanged superior smiles.

"The word 'Paradise' has miraculous powers," observed the young woman.

"It's a sort of universal password," her husband added.

"Tell me everything you know about him," urged Clément. "I've come a long way to make his acquaintance."

"Knowledge has always been an obsession with Westerners, hasn't it?" sneered Julien. "So-called knowledge — and the willingness to force it on others . . ."

"The man addressing you is Clément Calderanz," Nathalie broke in, speaking to Michelle. "The name means something to you, I believe. Do you think Clément Calderanz came all this way to play guessing games?"

I had not been expecting this sally, but the answer surprised me still more.

"We know perfectly well who we're dealing with," Michelle answered, unruffled. "But we're not in a Parisian drawing room here."

The contempt in her voice and the injustice of the remark were too much for me.

"So good of you to tell us," I said sourly. "In case you're interested, we've always avoided those places like the plague."

"But has it occurred to you that certain places might want to avoid *you?*" asked Julien.

He said it mildly, with no obvious wish to offend me. But I had lost whatever patience I had left. "Excuse us," I jeered. "We don't want to be pushy. Where have we left our good manners? We'll leave right away."

"As you please," the young man answered indifferently. "It no longer matters."

I was already picking up my pack, but I had reckoned without Clément; he had no intention of giving up.

He was sweating profusely; his eyes were ablaze, the way they had been on the first days of our trip. "You've found out something, haven't you?" he said, breathing heavily. "I know you're on to something."

Michelle merely shrugged.

"What can White people find out so far from home, except what they've brought with them in their baggage?" asked Julien.

What was he getting at? I could see that Nathalie was as perplexed as I was.

Reluctantly the teacher decided to elaborate. "This island has a peculiarity that sets it apart from its neighbors," he began. "Mixed blood is almost unknown here."

He was right. Physically, the island population was closer to its ancestral Africa than to the usual Caribbean grab bag of races; we would certainly have noticed it ourselves if our minds hadn't been clouded by other concerns.

"The people here," Julien went on, "never came to terms with our so-called civilization. It amuses them to watch White people play at being White people without even realizing they're on show. The consul warned us. Remember what he said — his exact words — 'It's a very different kind of show they're putting on now!' The nasty little myth of the happy-go-lucky darky is over. From now on it's us Whites who are on stage."

And Michelle: "The same as a hundred years ago during the uprising."

Calderanz was drinking in their words. He was hugely excited. "Yes! That's right! That's how it is!" he shouted. "We're the puppets and Paradise is pulling the strings!"

"Unwittingly," Julien went on, "we have all become the characters in a huge pantomime. Us, you, many others. The Blacks simply suggested the themes to us — the myth of the

dangerous, mysterious north, for example. Then they sat back
and watched us wriggle. A little flick of the finger every now and
then if we stopped twitching. Nothing at all really: a little wild
laughter, a few bushes rustling noisily, a few shots fired in the air,
a little chicken blood sprinkled over a broken-down bookmobile.
Our imaginations did the rest. None of it matters anymore."

"The Mirror Swamp!" Clément burst out. "Of course! They
were holding a mirror up to us. We claim to be writers, yet we
don't even know enough to take words at face value!"

He looked at Nathalie and me in triumph. "Didn't I tell you?
This Paradise is a genius of a director!"

The volunteer teachers greeted this remark with simultaneous
sighs.

"So you still haven't grasped a thing?" asked Michelle
disgustedly.

"You claim to be a writer, as you just said, but you can't even
liberate yourself from appearances," Julien said with amazement. "White you were the day you arrived in St. Elizabeth and
White you've remained."

But Clément was no longer listening to him. "The only writer
worthy of the name," he pontificated, "is the one who can pin
down the reality in a snare of appearances. Do you understand?
Your Paradise may never have written a line in his life, but he's the
greatest storyteller of them all!"

The young woman turned away, as if giving up all attempts to
make him see the light. Julien opened and closed his mouth
several times before he finally spoke. "I thought we had made
ourselves clear," he muttered. "Anyway, it doesn't matter anymore whether you understand or not."

He was back on the same old theme for the third time; I felt
my blood boil.

"Damn it," I growled. "Are you going to spill what's on your
mind or not?"

"Please," Nathalie added very gently.

"What's the point?" the young man sighed. "But if you
insist . . ."

He approached Calderanz and looked him straight in the eye. "Colonel Paradise is neither 'ours,' nor yours, nor anyone else's. There is not and there never was a Colonel Paradise. Like the north, the Mirror Swamp, Concession Eighteen — like all the mysterious hints and all the red herrings — he's just another of the island's mirages. In reality, he's nothing more nor less than the two words that make up his name, than the lies that have built his legend, than all the characteristics, qualities, and attributes you yourselves have given him. I'm sorry, Mr. Calderanz, but you're the only storyteller here."

"Me? Me?" (There was terror on Clément's face.) "I didn't create a thing!" He seemed petrified. "No," he muttered again. "Not me. I'm not the author."

"In that case," said the young man with a careless wave of the hand, "you've simply been a character in a novel written by nobody."

"The book of illusion and absence," Michelle remarked, without, I believe, realizing the cruelty of her words. "The book of shipwreck," stammered Clément.

He collapsed onto the nearest pew.

He suddenly looked like a little old man, his face livid, his pupils dead. Frail, or rather brittle, vulnerable to the slightest breath of wind.

"The dead man . . ." Now the Indian's words came back to me like a prophecy. Something had just died inside Clément Calderanz; the breath of life itself, desire, striving, the mad but sublime refusal to submit to the inevitable.

And I, just as suddenly, was deaf once more to savagery, to the call of the wild . . . Yet I had to do something to save the man who had been my best friend.

Michelle and Julien avoided looking at him, as if the sight of this stricken man was vaguely indecent. Nathalie sat down beside him, put an arm around his shoulders, and murmured something in his ear.

"Clément is exhausted," she said to us. "It's the reaction to all the upheavals and hardships of the last few days. Is there somewhere he can rest?"

"I'll show you the room we intended for you," said Julien.

They left the hall by a side door. The schoolteacher led the way. Nathalie struggled along behind him, supporting a dazed Calderanz who allowed himself to be steered, leaning all his weight against her. From the look that passed between us, I realized she wanted no help, however difficult the task. It occurred to me that she was honoring a contract she had made with herself.

I remained alone with Michelle, who had taken advantage of the interval to return quietly to her book. I suppose that from her point of view, everything had been said. In fact, I too wanted to believe that no more questions were necessary. But I lacked the fortitude to keep my mouth shut.

I walked to the edge of the stage. "I would like you to answer one question, Michelle," I said. "I saw your disapproving look just now when Clément collapsed. Do you think he's committed some crime? If so, I'd like to know how. Please, I really want to know."

"Crime?" she murmured. "Isn't everything that has ever happened on this island the crime of the White race?"

She couldn't get off the subject; I was talking to a wall: was there any point in going on? But once again I felt too weary, too disenchanted, to listen to the voice of moderation. I returned to the attack. "Until further notice," I replied sharply, "you and your husband are also a part of the system you find so loathsome."

She smiled a wintry smile. "You mean we have no place here either? I agree. But we can at least choose our camp. Otherwise, what would be the use of what we have learned? And do you really think we would be any more at home in France now? That we could go back there and teach things contrary to our beliefs?"

"Reading, writing, arithmetic?"

"You know very well it has nothing to do with that! I mean the ethos of the White man, the culture that is simply an alibi for arrogance and oppression."

"Forgive me, but those are very high-minded words for a very threadbare idea."

"You can think what you like. But you can't alter the fact that White men profane everything. What they call their civilization is simply a form of putrefaction . . ." (suddenly animated, she threw me a superior look implying knowledge that I, in my bewilderment, had no access to) "but they themselves are the first to putrefy!"

Julien had come back. "With independence," he said, "the rats left the ship. The Whites deserted this island in droves. Those who stayed didn't stay out of love. A few were kept here by their jobs. The others . . ." He sighed.

"The others?"

"Stuck in their ruts by gangrene. Moral gangrene."

"It's taken you quite a while to notice!" I sneered.

I was still determined to get the full story from them and wanted them to know that I wasn't going to be drawn into their game.

"We played our parts as Whites," said Michelle stiffly. "It was inevitable."

"The White man," her husband declared, "is obsessed by the ideas of History and Progress. For him, things have to move. He demands movement. And the people here gave it to him . . ."

"Which still doesn't explain your own spectacular . . . redemption."

They exchanged a questioning look.

"They opened our eyes," Julien said reluctantly, after an oppressive silence.

" 'They?' "

"We told you about Father Van Doren. We saw him again. He had changed. He arrived here last Tuesday or Wednesday with supplies and a little cash for us. Naturally, it was easier for him to find us than for you . . ."

"He told us everything," the young woman took up the thread. "The myth of the Mirror Swamp and of Colonel Paradise and all the rest . . . All the inducements they wave under White people's noses for the pleasure of watching them ape themselves . . ."

"But usually," said Julien, "that was exactly what the tourists wanted. They went scrambling back up the gangplank of the *Cornhill Missionary* with a delicious thrill of terror. It was our arrival that upset everything."

"The idea of government," Michelle continued, "is a White man's obsession. One more mirage among so many. It's been a long time since anything of the kind existed on St. Elizabeth. They scarcely even bother to keep up appearances anymore. And so—despite all our papers, our stamps, our official signatures—no one was expecting us and no one knew what to do with us. Two wide-eyed innocents can very quickly become troublesome witnesses. They did everything they could to get rid of us, but, since we were too stupid to understand, they decided to banish us to the bush, after a last attempt at intimidation by the priest himself had failed."

"Maybe you're going to tell me Van Doren is Black? I happen to have met him myself, you know."

Once again they exchanged inquiring looks.

"Of course you've met him!" Julien exclaimed. "The man's story comes close to being tragic, but it's a cautionary tale in more ways than one. He managed to be loyal and disloyal to everyone at once."

"He betrayed both camps," Michelle cut in. "He couldn't return to St. Elizabeth. For him there was no way out. The party was over. He wrenched us out of our idiotic dreamworld, and then he too had to face the truth."

"The truth?"

"Putrefaction! Decomposition!"

"What do you mean?"

The young man shrugged. "What do I mean? Come with me."

He led the way to a door in the back wall of the stage, under the great horseshoe stairway that climbed to the second floor of the house.

I followed him down a dark corridor to a second door.

Night had fallen, but the moonlight was bright enough to make my flashlight unnecessary.

Inside the room we had just entered — the room where the bough of the giant tree outside had broken through the window — the air was unbreathable.

From the branch dangled a human fruit that was slowly starting to liquefy.

The teacher leaned against the doorjamb. I turned to look at him, my scalp tingling as if pierced by a thousand needles, but he merely said nonchalantly: "He knew you would be here sooner or later. He knew your names. None of it matters in the least anymore."

He pulled a sheaf of papers from a pocket. "He left a letter for you."

## ⋆ *30* ⋆

Hendrik Van Doren had been twenty-nine, and considered a craftsman of great promise, when he suddenly decided to leave his uncle's workshop in Leiden to go into the church. His coworkers, who had liked his outgoing nature as much as they admired his skill, took up a collection for him; his uncle sold them some platinum at a quarter of its market price, and they fashioned an austerely beautiful pectoral cross for him as a farewell gift.

By chance, his first parish was Philipsburg in the Dutch half of St. Martin Island, which a historical caprice had split between the Netherlands and France. He acquitted himself more than honorably there, and, since he had used his stay on the island to perfect his knowledge of French, he was entrusted a few years later with a much more delicate mandate.

This was to establish a mission in St. Elizabeth, a sphere of Catholic influence where it was also likely that pagan cults had survived. But Van Doren's faith burned all the fiercer because it had come to him late and had been born of skepticism.

However, he soon had to acknowledge that he would get nowhere by concentrating his efforts on the city, where worship was at best a social convention, an excuse for the few faithful to gather and pass their Sunday leisure time. With the concurrence of his superiors, he therefore decided to prospect the interior of the island. When he proposed building a church, the colonial administration of the day suggested that he save his money and take over Paradise House, which needed nothing more than a few repairs. Only later did he suspect that papist rivalry was behind this offer — which kept him isolated in the heart of the Mirror Swamp.

Nonetheless, he transformed the mansion's spacious reception hall into a church, with the use of a few pews and a raised stage. He then plunged into the task of attracting souls concerned for their salvation, if any were to be found . . . He was ready to fight with all his might, to make any sacrifice in furtherance of this sacred endeavor. Unfortunately, the road to heaven did not seem to be the chief concern of most of the souls he had to contend with. A dozen or so Blacks, never the same ones, attended services, perhaps out of pity but probably out of curiosity. A year later, their number had dwindled by half. Finally there came a Sunday when Van Doren found himself staring at a single parishioner, who fled as soon as the priest addressed him.

He should have been distressed; but he realized that deep down he was immensely relieved. This realization staggered him. Since his arrival in St. Elizabeth he had been a helpless witness of the island's spiritual decline. Through long, sleepless nights he had prayed that his lost sheep would find a glimmer of light in the depths of their night. Now that same night was invading his own beliefs! His heart had imperceptibly given up struggling against Black apathy and White abdication. He still did not understand these people, but he was forced to admit — and it was a horrible admission — that he could no longer condemn or even pity them. For he, too, as soon as the ability to sleep was restored to him, had begun to lose all hope in humanity.

The change had come over him imperceptibly; and now, like them, he no longer even hoped that confidence might return to him someday. He realized that belief in God meant nothing in a priest, if he no longer believed in man.

He closed the church and put the platinum cross away in a drawer.

He felt neither affection nor dislike for the islanders. For months on end, he was his only company—and this was not a source of consolation. From time to time he called on the Indian storekeeper or visited the souvenir stores in the capital, which he supplied with various handcrafted trinkets. As in his youth, his manual skills earned him a living. His reproductions of Carib axes, in particular, were enormously popular with tourists.

He no longer even opened the mail from his bishop. When that worthy man, troubled by his silence, came to visit him, he hid in the forest, warned beforehand of his superior's arrival.

On the other hand, he made an exception to his general misanthropic rule for the man who—from the best of motives— had warned him of the bishop's presence among the *Cornhill Missionary*'s passengers: none other than old man Lombardi. The former consul's rich store of gossip and lore amused Van Doren, who gladly killed time with him at the bar of the Christophe-Liberté whenever he dropped in.

"Reality per se does not exist!" the old maniac would trumpet. "Reality is a creation of the mind. It is poetry, my dear fellow: a magnificent hallucination!"

For all too short a time, his companion could forget his failures, his despair, the shame of his denial.

Then came independence, and with it a sense of accelerating degradation, for he saw himself reflected in the handful of White men who stayed behind and whose apathy and inertia seemed to embody the decline of the West.

The wound was further poisoned when a new breed of Whites began to descend on St. Elizabeth, a breed sure of its rights if unconvinced of its virtues, the kind of Whites who believed in the genius of their race and the future of their civilization: the kind of Whites who had not succumbed to the island's malevolent pranks and who breathlessly extolled its Garden of Eden charms.

Like the rest of the European colony, the priest hated these tourists. Most of all he hated seeing himself through their own eyes (a feeling that was aggravated by his envy of people still capable of pride and illusions). He became obsessed with the need to put a dent in their complacency. Lombardi's ravings soon suggested how this might be done. And so, on a hotel veranda one fine January morning, the tales of kidnapped tourists, of the terrifying north, and of the vicious Colonel Paradise were born as a sinister practical joke.

The effect of these revelations on the first tourists to hear them was so devastating that they almost trampled each other in their rush to get back aboard ship. The news spread like wildfire through the small White community, despite the fact that its social network had declined considerably. Everyone was delighted with the joke, a richly deserved revenge on the snobbish, pretentious "mainlanders." What's more, it put a decisive halt to their humiliating inquisitiveness. From then on, tourists would be denied the pleasure of telling people what they had seen on the island—since they would no longer be seeing anything.

Encouraged by this vote of confidence, Van Doren returned to his game of mystification the very next day; his success was abetted by the complicity of White residents at neighboring tables, who eagerly confirmed his stories, adding details of their own that were guaranteed to make their listeners' hair stand on end.

When these rumors reached Lombardi, somewhere between islands in the archipelago, he recognized in them the confirmation of his own personal brand of metaphysics. He not only was quickly convinced himself of the colonel's existence, but even ended up imagining that his own henchman Joseph had fought under the colonel in several guerrilla actions during the movement for independence (actions that had in fact taken place only inside Lombardi's cracked skull). Joseph, who valued his job, denied nothing.

Soon every White resident was adding his own brick to the edifice. Refining, snipping, fine-tuning, chiseling, they constantly came up with new details. In truth, it was nothing more than a new kind of handicraft; it absorbed the priest and his accomplices so thoroughly that it took them several weeks to notice that the Blacks in their turn had embraced the myth.

They did more: they conferred on it a texture that was all their own. They invented a whole series of pantomimes and skits to buttress the tourists' belief in the whispers they heard in the gloomy dampness of the Christophe-Liberté. The town became a vast orgy of sidelong glances, of ominous silences, of zombie faces at every street corner, of vaguely outlandish shapes attaching themselves to your heels as if trailing you.

On the island, independence had not triggered the vast popular enthusiasm shown on other islands. Independence Day celebrations were more like a formality, hastily executed amid general indifference. There had been no resurgence of interest in politics in its wake. There had been no ground swell of political parties, no factional squabbling. As in the past, observers reported empty polling stations on election day. The government put in power by this "electoral process" returned to its anonymity as furtively as it had emerged from it, and remained there, utterly inaccessible. It would have been hard to identify a single measure carried out in its name. Total, permanent recess seemed to be the order of the day in the gloomy government buildings. A phantom state presided over lethargic institutions.

Life, more vegetable than animal in nature, somehow sustained itself (but for how long?) in this country on the margins of the world, indifferent to the larger stakes of history, unconcerned with its own future.

Given this state of affairs, who could have suspected that a simple practical joke would kindle a flame that no ideal had ever been able to light? Yet that is what happened. The flame had mysteriously flickered out of the ashes of desire and hope; very quickly it was fanned into a blaze.

Once he had got over his surprise, the priest was awestruck at this unforeseen awakening. Perhaps he had become discouraged too easily . . . What if this upheaval heralded the glimmers of redemption? What if, by creating the myth of the colonel, he had finally accomplished his priestly mission? What if the natives rediscovered faith in themselves and in him and confidence in humanity by following this unlikely path? What if they were about to reconcile themselves with God?

It was a dream larger than life, but one he desperately wanted to believe in. He broadcast his lies with the same intensity with which he had once held divine services. The same passion drove him to carve birds of paradise on his axe heads (rather crudely, for the sake of realism). Anything that contributed to the triumph of the myth, he believed, would lead to the healing of souls.

In a sense, his wish was granted. The myth became the island's soul, and that soul vibrated with pride.

How could anyone even call it mystification now? Scaring the tourists was merely a marginal aspect of the joke by this time. It paled into insignificance beside the fascination the fiction held for the islanders, even though they shared — and more than shared — responsibility for it with Van Doren. It was as if the imaginary exploits of Colonel Paradise were more real to them than the want and misery of their daily lives. They were finding their historical roots again along the pathways of fanaticism.

It was this paradox that ultimately forced the Dutchman to a truer appreciation of the situation. It was a bitter realization. All his exalted hopes went up in smoke. God hadn't returned to the island; nor would He deliver His priest from damnation.

The Black population had turned away from action — from life. Instead they had chosen this game, a game that, in the final disastrous analysis, perverted the very meaning of life. Van Doren had hoped for an awakening, a happy evolution: but the myth had turned out to be nothing but an excuse for immobility in every conceivable domain. Such a disposition to inertia presupposed that these people no longer expected anything, either in this world or the next. So, Van Doren now saw, their attachment to the game proceeded from a monstrous act of blasphemy.

Horrified by this realization, the priest fled to his church, hoping that God would appear to him in one form or another and show him the path he must follow. But he encountered only silence inside the mansion's ancient walls. Silence, and the crushing sense of his own guilt.

The very name of the place, the attitude of the natives in the neighboring villages, all reminded him painfully that he was the author of this fable over which he had lost all semblance of control.

He went out and sat on the broken flagstones of the terrace; there, he thought over the major events of his life and saw, or thought he saw, that destiny had mocked him. One word, it seemed to him, perfectly summed up everything that had shaped his experience: blindness. And now, as if by accident, he himself was purveying blindness. Blindness in the hoodwinked tourists; blindness in the island's Whites, who believed they could hide their degradation behind this frail screen of deception; blindness in the Blacks, who were spellbound by a story they repeated tirelessly to one another, convincing themselves that it was more real than reality itself. Four forms of alienation, if he included his own. Four ways of looking at the world through a blindfold.

As he turned all this over in his mind, the picture of the blindfolded reader came to him. He took the platinum cross from the drawer where he had put it and went to the blacksmith in the nearest village. He built an earth mold. A masterpiece of miniaturization. He melted down the cross. Using the lost-wax technique, he poured the molten metal into the matrix of hardened clay. Then, with a file, he painstakingly finished the figure.

Since the process made it essential to destroy the mold each time, he had to make a new one for every statuette. He worked for as long as his supply of platinum lasted. By the evening of the second day, he had used it all up.

The whole village watched every step of the operation without uttering a word. Van Doren selected the best proportioned of all the statuettes and thrust it into his pocket. The rest he offered to the Indian storekeeper at a price absurdly lower than their real value. The Indian protested vigorously. He had no wish to help promote the sale of profane wares. But the priest left the consignment with him and set off for St. Elizabeth the next morning.

On the way, he wondered why he had decided to bind the figurine's hands. It had come to him as a sudden inspiration, and he had obeyed without a second's thought. Now he was astonished at the uncanny rightness of his intuition. Without that last detail, the allegory would have been incomplete.

For the island was indeed the captive of its myth. It was condemned to give flesh and blood to the myth or the myth would turn against it. And he and the other Whites were also imprisoned by their lie, now that the Blacks had appropriated it from them. If they attempted to reestablish the truth at this late date, there was now a whole arsenal of tangible proofs to contradict them. Supposing, of course, that the Blacks would tolerate such a recantation.

But what Van Doren still did not know was how dangerous all such speculation had become. In the next few days the local Europeans noticed that letter carriers were withholding their overseas mail (which had always been at the mercy of the post office's lunatic whims). When their correspondence arrived at all, it left no doubt that it had been closely scrutinized. An unseen hand cut off phone conversations as soon as they touched on certain subjects. As time went on, the personal phone lines of the Whites became subject to chronic breakdown. Poker-faced officials listened stonily to their complaints until the complainants finally realized the futility of their efforts.

Shortly thereafter a sinister accident befell a former planter, a man who had gone into the café business after the massive expropriations of foreign property that followed independence. One day he was a little too talkative with a group of tourists in his café (he was one of his own best customers). Several witnesses stated that he told them they were about as likely to meet Colonel Paradise on the island as to meet Santa Claus. The next day he vanished while out hunting. He was last seen heading down the trail toward the old hospital, his rifle slung, his birddog at his heels. That was all the subsequent inquiry — a rather languid affair — was able to unearth. When his barmaid started to worry about his absence and his friends went off to look for him, they found no trace of man, gun, or dog.

As a result of this episode the White community realized, as Van Doren had a little earlier, that they were now the hostages of their own hoax and that denying the myth meant they risked seeing it enacted *at their expense*. The conclusion was ironic but crystal clear: to protect themselves from the myth, they had to go on propagating it.

The priest threw himself into this task more strenuously than anyone else. Out of self-mockery, no doubt. But also out of a feeling that, because he was more responsible than the others, he needed to drive away as many visitors as possible so he wouldn't have the burden of another disappearance on his conscience.

The arrival of the young French teachers caught him, like everyone else in the capital, off guard. They were not tourists. The contract that had brought them to St. Elizabeth expressly forbade them to leave. Uncertain what to do, the priest chose to avoid them. He even retreated to Paradise House, hoping against hope that by the time he returned to St. Elizabeth the young couple would have disappeared.

Unfortunately, they hung on and seemed to take root. Yet they were hounded mercilessly, for they were the most receptive audience the natives had ever had. The day he returned to the city the Dutchman learned that the authorities were exiling them to the bush. In other words, to an area where they might easily get wind of the plot—which would have been their death sentence. How could he persuade them to disobey? How could he warn them of what lay ahead? He was himself under close surveillance: since his return he had been shadowed night and day by several guardian angels.

Not unreasonably, his solution was to give the couple an even more terrifying picture of the north. That would give Black eavesdroppers the illusion that he was playing their game, while at the same time warning the couple—at least he had to hope it would—of the risk they were running.

He made only one mistake: in his eagerness to get his message across, he overacted his part so much that the young people took him for a crackpot and avoided him like the plague.

Shattered by this new defeat, Van Doren was left alone with his bitterness and remorse under the suspicious gaze of spies who didn't let him out of their sight for a second.

But, as the months went by, news of the young couple continued to trickle in. Encouraging news. The youngsters seemed to be confining their activities to the southern half of the island. Perhaps they had heeded him after all.

He began to hope again. But not for long.

The diffident little man who carried out the duties of consul on behalf of French citizens announced that he and his wife were leaving for Europe. A few days later both died from mysterious causes. It was whispered that they had been poisoned.

These two deaths, following so soon on the café owner's disappearance, were too much for the priest. Yet he still had not reached the bottom of the abyss. For at that very juncture we — Nathalie, Clément, Paul, and I — stepped ashore from the *Cornhill Missionary*. Our stated aim: to follow the old Slave Trail.

He had to stop us at any price. Unfortunately, forced once again to mislead the waiters at the Christophe-Liberté, he went about it in such a way that he merely fanned the flames of Clément's excitement. Once again, he had missed the chance to redeem himself. But this was once too often.

As a last desperate resort, he slipped the blindfolded reader into my palm, hoping halfheartedly that I, since I seemed more sensible than Clément, would be able to crack the statuette's code.

We had set off along the Trail. He had followed our progress without difficulty: we were the sole topic of conversation in town, and it was as if a team of reporters had joined our expedition. The same channels informed him about the teachers' sudden change of itinerary, the bookmobile's breakdown, the macabre charade it had inspired, and all the events that followed.

As a final stroke of bad luck, a rumor began to go the rounds: all these White people straying north of Three-and-Two-Clouds were to be rounded up and brought to a place where it would be easy to make them disappear — for good. The place: Paradise House, his church, the church he had deserted.

He did not wait to hear more. This time he had reached the end of his tether. He had gone through anguish, terror, distress, utter despair. There was nothing that could hurt him anymore. Somehow he would rescue us from our fate. He was prepared to sacrifice his own life in the attempt.

So Van Doren approached the skipper of the *Cornhill Missionary* (who had long been intrigued by the tales his passengers brought back up the gangplanks with them) and told him the whole story. He made a detailed confession in the presence of Lombardi and of several Europeans who in one way or another were the official representatives of their respective countries. By coincidence, a reporter and a photographer were also on board that day, putting together a Caribbean report for a big California paper.

By the time the priest was through, the myth of Colonel Paradise was an empty, crumpled paper bag. When they learned of this betrayal, the Blacks were forced to accept their powerlessness. There was no longer any question of harming a hair on our heads. We were taboo — which explained why we had been left in perfect peace since the axe episode.

Van Doren was convinced that he had signed his own death warrant. But he soon realized that, on the contrary, his confession protected him from reprisals. For the last time, he took a boat and headed up the coast for the great house where the heady vision of his youth had been transformed into a leering nightmare. He immediately realized that, although Michelle and Julien were drinking in his every word, they were still incapable of understanding what he was trying to tell them.

They in turn were full of illusions, full of their obtuse and suicidal "understanding" of the island, the same "understanding" he had once boasted of. He knew from experience that it would do no good to lecture them.

But it was one more defeat, and he had already paid too dearly for his mistakes. Tortured by guilt, convinced he had earned eternal damnation, he decided to end his life on earth. Since he would never be able to wipe his mind clean of the terrible events in which he had been both actor and spectator, he might as well obliterate that mind. And there was another thing: by coming to our rescue, he had condemned the island to fall back into its former stagnation; he had uprooted from it the little that still survived there of the ideal, however aberrant its form. Of all his crimes, this seemed to him the most unforgivable.

His letter closed with this line, underlined in a shaky hand: "I love God with all my might, but I can no longer believe in His love."

★ 31 ★

Driven by the stench, and by the gloom that invaded the room as soon as it started to rain again, I had gone back into the old chapel to read this painful story.

When I returned, the big reception hall was deserted. A single bulb, hanging naked from its wire and encrusted with insect corpses, threw a sepulchral light on the scene.

Folding the thick sheaf of papers, I thought about all the common threads linking the destinies of Hendrik Van Doren and Clément Calderanz. Each had denied something he had later striven vainly but desperately to rediscover. Inspiration for one; divine providence for the other. Something that was supposed to justify at last all his efforts, and at the same time utterly repudiate them.

I was stuffing the letter into my pocket when Nathalie came in. She looked at me for a moment, her face graver than I had ever seen it. I was incapable of breaking the silence: too many ambiguities, doubts, suspicions, and regrets now walled me off from her.

"He is very ill," she said in a faint voice. "He has asked for you several times."

A number of details in the room to which she led me indicated that this had been the priest's bedroom when he had lived in the house. Clément lay on a narrow camp bed so low the mattress seemed to be touching the floor. The tiny room was lit by resin candles whose struggling flames were periodically blown flat by the wind. As I stopped on the threshold, they put my shadow through a wild series of gymnastics on the ceiling and walls.

My heart was gripped in a tight vise. I could have sworn that Clément Calderanz's face was more emaciated than ever, as if his very being were slowly draining out of him. But he looked more like the old Clément now than at any time since his hair had been cut.

He smiled at me, and his smile, more mischievous than sarcastic, also took us back to the old days.

"Ah, Tommy!" he said in a weak voice. "What a fool I've been, haven't I? What a poor fool!"

Surprised by this approach, I probably frowned.

"No, no, you're right, as usual. Not a poor fool, a dangerous fool. Lord! But good triumphs in the end: I'm reaping as I sowed. I wanted to write a story with my own life as raw material, and all I've managed to do is turn my life into a ludicrous moral lesson. To turn myself—when all I really sought was the secret springs of the imagination—into a character in a fable. Not even the reflection of a pale imitation of Don Quixote—because I didn't tilt at windmills, Tom, I merely dreamed of them."

"This island is no dream," I said, my mind still on the priest's confession.

"Yes. I was the nightmare . . . Listen, old friend, I want you to forgive me."

"Nobody forced me to follow you, Clément."

"I wasn't thinking of that. You have to forgive me for what I said to you this afternoon on the beach. Nathalie has explained it all to me."

Explained what? I turned to the young woman, but her eyes were imploring me to say nothing.

"There's nothing to forgive," I muttered. "You're my best friend, Clément."

He smiled again. "Yes, I know. I know that now. The story is ending on a truly tame note, isn't it? I should have taken Colonel

Paradise's place, I should have put myself in that phantom's skin and given him life. But I no longer have the strength. My face can't take any more masks. My mind is clear again. Which is the worse punishment, Tommy: knowledge or blindness?" And without pausing he added: "Your story . . . is it going well?"

I lowered my head.

"Don't worry," he continued. "I'm not weeping over my fate. I even have a powerful consolation. Do you remember, in Paris, when I was picking the pockets of every good author in sight in hopes of finding *the key?* There's a Hemingway line I remember by heart."

"On war and writing?"

"No, not that one. But it's basically on the same theme — experience versus esthetics. It was about Joseph Conrad and T. S. Eliot. Hemingway wrote: 'If I knew that by grinding Mr. Eliot into a fine dry powder and sprinkling that powder over Mr. Conrad's grave, Mr. Conrad would shortly reappear, looking very annoyed at the forced return, and commence writing, I would leave for London early tomorrow morning with a sausage grinder.'"

"I know the line," I said.

"Well, Tom, I thought I would find Mr. Conrad's grave here. I was wrong. But I still managed to reduce an esthete to powder. The one who fires first dies first, remember? Peace to the ashes of Clément Calderanz."

A little before four in the morning he breathed his last. I use that antiquated expression deliberately, for it very accurately describes what I saw. At that moment, my friend gently closed his eyes, pressed his lips together, and held his breath for eternity.

Nathalie and I went on looking at him, she leaning against the wall and I squatting at the foot of the bed. The wind had dropped, but the rain still pattered down on the foliage outside.

A long time later the young woman went to the window and said: "I believe I always knew it. I guessed it would end like this the moment this journey was mentioned. Inspiration is one of the names men give to what they will never find. Men like him. The day he danced with the natives and they drew away from him, I knew I was right. I remembered what the Abbé Descamps had written about the gift attributed to the Blacks on this island, the gift of foreseeing someone's death."

Michelle and Julien showed even less surprise, and no distress at all. Van Doren had been right: they were prisoners of the island and its spells.

They did not lift a finger to help us. Clément rests beside the priest among the roots of the great tree. He remained in the land of his dreams, fertilizing it with the fiction that had been his life.

★ *32* ★

When we looked for them, to say good-bye, the teachers were nowhere to be found. But I had the feeling they were watching us, hidden somewhere in the vegetation that still dripped under a thin sun scarcely less pallid than the sky.

We borrowed the priest's boat and reached the capital early in the afternoon.

Our baggage, apparently intact, was still waiting for us at the Christophe-Liberté. Two patrol boats and a frigate, flying the flags of France, the Netherlands, and the United States, respectively, were standing offshore: Van Doren's report had been taken seriously. A veil of silence seemed to have fallen over the town. The streets were empty. The hotel staff, reduced to three, moved about furtively, in an atmosphere of ruin and funereal gloom. Sheepish, shamefaced, they avoided our eyes. Even behind the shelter of his desk, the receptionist acted like a man afraid of being struck.

Along with our things, he handed us a big manila envelope addressed to Nathalie.

It contained Paul's manuscript—that "tapestry of fugitive gleams and muted murmurs"—to which a short note had been stapled.

Nathalie and I had not exchanged a single word since leaving Paradise House. Throughout the boat ride she had sat in the bow, staring straight ahead, while I steered from the stern. I had taken advantage of my isolation to drop Hendrik Van Doren's figurine surreptitiously into the waves, along with the account of his tribulations.

I did my best to banish all the questions I was burning to ask about Clément. Hadn't I already tried to fathom too many mysteries, and only made myself more miserable and more isolated than ever?

But as soon as she was given Paul's letter, everything in my heart suddenly boiled over.

"Nathalie," I said, "why did you kiss him? Why did you lie to Clément? What did you tell him about us?"

Calmly, she tore up Paul's message, spread the pieces in the biggest ashtray in the bar, and held a match to them.

"Let's walk a little," she said when it had all burned away.

The sun's splendor had returned, tinting the dead streets of St. Elizabeth the same diffident gold it sometimes gilds the streets of Paris I loved so much. Leaving the shuttered storefronts behind us, we strolled in the direction of the port.

"I always had the tenderest feelings for Paul," she began. "He was so vulnerable. All of us were, of course, but he couldn't even hide it . . . I suppose I didn't handle him too skillfully. He got it into his head that I felt something more than affection for him. While we were in Paris he never tried to push his supposed advantage. You know why, Tommy? Because he was convinced that he had to deserve me, that he couldn't take me away from Clément unless he managed to outstrip him as a writer. He knew how much I admired my husband's work. But once he wrote that story, once he saw how moved I was when he read it to us, he decided he had passed the test and could declare himself. He asked me to his room, said we couldn't put off talking any longer. I had a pretty good idea what it would be about, but I went anyway, thinking it would give me a chance to set him straight. Unfortunately, Clément saw me go in and drew the conclusions he mentioned to you."

"He should have trusted you," I said. "Didn't he know you?"

"He no longer trusted himself. That was his sickness. Tommy, I want you to understand. He said he was sick—and in his mouth that was no metaphor. This whole business wasn't just about his mind. Doubt had attacked his very roots: ever since the publication of his essay he had been a diminished man, physically diminished."

"You don't mean—"

"I suffered along with him. I tried to reassure him. Believe me, I tried everything. But despite my efforts he imagined I was turning away from him. And the worst part, you see, was that a gulf actually was beginning to open between us. Because I lacked the courage to cross it—and it grew wider every day. You lived through that period; you know what he was like. I too felt rebuffed. And the more distance he put between us the guiltier I felt about what was happening to us, because I could no longer love him the way I did before. My guilt feelings, added to his own, merely hastened the break. I ended up wondering whether he hadn't read his own diagnosis somewhere deep inside me— whether I hadn't been the cause of this crisis."

"The cause?"

"Please let me go on. The trouble with Paul was that our conversation left him convinced that I had lied to him, that I secretly did love him. The day we visited the Forcerie he tried to get me to admit it. Once again, all my denials were useless. So a little later, realizing he would never give up his illusions, I took him out to the ruins near the filling station. There I told him that I had never been in love with him, that I never would be, that I loved somebody else, and that I would give him a kiss that would be the first and last thing he would ever obtain from me. A kiss of peace; a kiss of farewell in final settlement of his vain hopes."

"God!" I murmured. "And I thought . . ."

"I hoped he wouldn't insist. I wanted him to go back to St. Elizabeth. This expedition was physically beyond him, and it was no concern of his. But all I managed to do was reinforce his illusions. After that, my only recourse was to break with him brutally. Although it hurt me to do so, I behaved in the only way that might open his eyes. I drew nearer to Clément. I was as hard and unfeeling as I could be. And finally, as a last resort, I stole your compass and maps."

"What I don't understand," I said, "is why Clément didn't pull himself together at that point. He had no more reason to be jealous. He had told me that he wanted to win you back, that that was his deepest motive: hadn't he succeeded?"

She looked at me almost shyly, then stared thoughtfully at the ground beneath her feet. "You know," she went on, after a moment's silence, without answering my question, "there was one thing I wanted more than anything else: for him to realize how much I wanted him to succeed, even if, deep down inside me, I was convinced he only wanted to destroy himself. Why couldn't he stop hating himself? I asked you that question one day, Tom, and I haven't been able to get it out of my silly mind since. Clément was one of the best writers in the world, perhaps the greatest of them all in his own field. That's what I've always thought and what I still think. Ah! Tommy, nobody, not even Clément, could ever know what Clément Calderanz meant to me . . . When I read him for the first time, years before our marriage, the shock I felt seemed like something I had been expecting all my life. No, that's not quite right: I felt that every single one of the flimsy threads that form the fabric of this life had suddenly been woven together. They started at a precise spot and moved along a precise path to depict a face that was mine, a face that suddenly (just when I had given up hope) revealed all its true meaning. That was the effect the book had on me. I actually existed. I discovered what I had been and what I wanted to become. Thanks to Clément Calderanz, my intelligence, my awareness, came into their own. My body as well. And they belonged only to me. To me and to him, if he wanted them. But the years go by, Tommy . . . Something is destroyed despite our best efforts."

She stopped talking. We had come to the jetty, deserted like the rest of the town, solitary like a Thelonious Monk melody. We stopped to gaze at the sky: on the far horizon, beyond the patrolling warships, mysterious green lights glowed like the highlights in a glass of absinthe.

"Nathalie," I said, when I realized I had to speak. "Why didn't you tell him all this yesterday on the beach? Why didn't you tell him you loved him?"

"Why? Well . . . I guess Clément isn't likely to find out now. I put all his doubts to rest: I owed him that at least. So I suppose you should know the truth. You want to know why, Tommy?"

She turned her whole body toward me and looked deeply and fearlessly into my eyes. "Because, just a moment before that, I had been about to say the same thing to another man. A man to whom I had already nearly admitted it, once before, on a path in the Luxembourg Gardens."

## * *Epilogue* *

Until I finally went back to my decaying Brooklyn neighborhood, we continued to meet occasionally. And, like the heroes of my fragile stories, I continued to keep silent.

There may be men who can capitalize on the victories they win despite themselves, but I'm not one of them. There are some deficiencies you can never overcome. And then, I felt, nothing could have matched the beauty of the feeling that had once revealed Nathalie to herself through the pages of a book.

At least that's what I tell myself every day. It's my way of continuing to believe in writing, continuing to invent a wonderful island for myself somewhere so I can go on writing.

But I'm not sure I'm right.

*Paris, Mérangle, Montreal*
*February 1982–March 1987*